HOT VAMPIRES

THE LORENA QUINN TRILOGY

SAMANTHA SNOW

Get Yourself a FREE Bestselling Paranormal Romance Book!

About This Book

When her grandmother passed away, 19 year old Lorena Quinn was left a small fortune in her will.

Along with a further surprise.

Upon accepting the inheritance, Lorena learned that she was central to a prophecy. A prophecy that forecast the end of the world and Lorena was the only one who could save it.

For this to happen, Lorena would have to have a child with one of the four sons of Vlad. Commonly known as vampires.

Now she has to choose which of the four eligible vampire bachelors will be the father of her child.

However, before she makes her choice, she must first live with them. All of them, at the same time...

Welcome To **The House Of Vampires!**

Things get very interesting in this vampire romance series aimed at adults. If you liked Vampire Diaries, True Blood, Twilight or anything that is sexy and paranormal then you will LOVE this!

For even the very wise cannot see all ends

-Tolkien

CHAPTER ONE

I should have been able to recognize my grandmother's house, even though I had never been there. They were all supposed to look pretty much the same, right? A picket fence, happy little mailbox, and lacy handmade curtains that fluttered in the middle of the midsummer breeze. Maybe there would be a fat dog or a moody cat lounging on a porch cluttered with the shoes of her many visiting grandchildren. My grandmother's house had none of these things. At least, not as far as I could see.

"You have got to be kidding me," I muttered under my breath.

I pulled my powder blue VW Bug into the tiny driveway, parked beneath the aluminum car port, and double checked the GPS on my phone to make sure that I hadn't taken a left turn for the Twilight Zone. 1730 Sparrow Field Lane, middle of nowhere Virginia. Yup. My phone, complete with Wonder Woman phone case, promised me that I was there. Okay, fine. Whatever. I turned off the navigation app and looked at the house, trying not to feel completely disappointed.

I must have pictured my grandmother's place a thousand times. I mean, my dad never really talked about her or anything, but I had always wondered about her. Who wouldn't? Especially since I didn't have a whole lot of family to start with, it was just me and dad, and we were always moving around, so I didn't have many friends either. Sometimes, I wondered if she was ridiculously rich, like Bill Gates rich, and that she was living in some super fancy place where you had to wear some kind of futuristic implant on the wrist just to get past security.

And sometimes I wondered if she was, like Dad said sometimes, crazy. That maybe her place was really the psych ward at a hospital. I have a really active imagination. Dad blames my choices in hobbies, but I blame my complete lack of friends.

The house, being nothing like I had imagined, was old and shabby, and it looked like it was going to fall right off the side of the mountain that it clung to. Once upon a time, it might have been a cute little rustic cottage, but it was a few decades beyond that. It was built with dark tree logs, cabin style, with a little porch that was decorated with what looked like ten different wind chimes, all made of different materials. There was no cute animal lounging in the sun or pile of kids' shoes. Just an old rocking chair with a single pillow so faded that I couldn't tell what the pattern had been.

"Jeez," I groaned as I opened up my car door, grabbed my lone box of possessions out of the passenger seat, and stepped out into the Appalachian sunshine. For October, it was pretty warm, still hovering in the mid-seventies with a heavy breeze; just cool enough for me to get away with wearing my jean jacket over a t-shirt, complete with screen-printed dragon, and jeans so worn they were almost white. I tugged the jacket closer and pulled a very crumpled envelope off the very top of the box.

The box was what I called "my stuff." '. My dad moved a lot for work. He's in district marketing. I didn't t know what that means, exactly, but it usually winds up with us going from one place to the next just as I start to feel settled in.

Since mom disappeared when I was little, I pretty much had to do whatever he said. My best friends when I was a kid were comics, books, and handheld video games. Don't judge; that stuff can keep you from getting lonely. My Stuff, capital letters please, was chock full of my favorite things: the things that I couldn't live without in case the moving van lost half of our worldly possessions...again.

Inside the envelope were three things. The first was a letter. It must have been folded and unfolded thirty times. I knew, because it had been me that did the folding. The creases in the paper were starting to come apart.

To Miss Lorena Meredith Quinn, the first line read. That was me, though I couldn't remember anyone ever calling me "Miss" unless they were really polite or really pissed. Sometimes both. I have that effect on people.

It is my duty, though not my pleasure, to inform you of the passing of Loretta Quinn, your grandmother, as of August 31st of this year. I am sorry for the late notice. We attempted to reach out to your father first, but received no response.

I snorted. Yeah, like my dad was ever going to respond to the death of the woman he was really busy pretending didn't exist.

Your grandmother has left all of her belongings to you: the house that she spent her life in and everything within it. Her savings, which totals to an amount of six hundred and eighty thousand dollars and thirty seven cents, is also to be passed on to you.

Cha-ching, I thought to myself, and then felt immediately guilty about it. Yeah, it was cool to suddenly have money, but I kind of would have preferred to meet my grandma. Still, a couple hundred thousand dollars was going to go a long way to paying off the student loans for that two-thirds of a year of college I had flunked out of and the credit card that I had already maxed out.

I'm not terrible with money, just throwing that out there. I am, or was, a minimum wage employee without health benefits and a totally broken arm last year. While my dad's insurance paid for most of it, it hadn't covered the time I couldn't work and the bills that I'd had to pay while hauling around a cast that weighed half as much as me, which is no small amount, thank you very much.

While no amount of money can replace the love that your grandmother had for you, it was stipulated in her will that in order for you to receive this inheritance, you must spend at least six months at her home in Colt Valley, Virginia. I hope to see you soon.

Marquessa Green

I folded up the letter and put it back in the envelope. The second item was a key, pretty much the same size and shape as a billion other house keys in America. The last was a picture, the kind from an old Polaroid camera. The glossy square showed a woman who couldn't have been more than fifty, holding a small child in her arms. Her ash-brown hair was coiled into a thick braid that trailed over one shoulder, and her nose was sharp and pointed. Basically, just like mine.

In a thick sharpie marker, someone had written on the white rectangle at the bottom, *"Loretta with Lorena, 3 mo old."*

It was the first picture of my grandmother that I had ever seen. There was something about the way the woman in the picture looked at the baby that made my throat feel too tight. Like she was just so sure that the little girl was going to amount to something. I am sorry to say that my grandmother would have been really disappointed. Unless she thought that a fast food working college dropout was the absolute best thing a girl could be. Then we'd be just fine. I doubted it though.

"Well," I said as I plucked the key out of the envelope, "here goes nothing."

I paused halfway to the side door. I had heard something, I was almost sure of it. A whisper, I thought. A woman's voice. I thought it had said my name. Then again, maybe I had just been imagining things. I had been driving for sixteen hours and living off drive-thru food. It was enough to make anyone hear things. That stuff is bad for you. Trust me, I know.

It took a little work, but I got the door open. Time or weather had made the fit imperfect. I had to use my hip, which was a little larger than I would have liked it to be, to bump open the door. It creaked ominously and swung away to give me my very first look at the woman that I had never known.

Messy was the first word that came to mind, or at least unorganized. I found myself smiling. My dad had always hated that I wasn't as much of a neat freak as he was, and now I knew why. The cabin wasn't gross; there weren't piles of food or anything, just a lot of clutter. I could see the kitchen and the living room from the doorway, as well as a tiny little nook that I guess you could call a dining room. All of the space was taken up by...stuff.

I stepped inside, not bothering to take my shoes off, and started to wander. Piles of magazines from twenty different years were tucked beneath a squat living room table with newspapers on top. I set my box of things next to the stacks and took a look around. There were three bookshelves in different heights cluttered with books, pictures, and what my dad would have called knickknacks. Mostly, they were bits of rock and crystal, but there were small piles of what looked like broken glass and metal, too. At first, I thought it was junk, but then I remembered all the wind chimes that were hanging outside. I scratched "junk" off of my mental list and wrote in "art supplies." Grandma was artsy; we had that in common, too. Or at least, we did before she had died.

I shook off the strange emotions that came with that thought and continued my exploration of the main room. The books were...weird. The ones that I could read had titles like "The Meaning of Dreams" and "Cleansing the Aura of Your House" and others that would have looked right at home in a new-age store. The rest were in languages that I didn't know, but I was guessing a couple were Latin. My grandmother was new-agey. Neat. We didn't have that in common. I wasn't religious or spiritual.

What surprised me most were the pictures. Most of them were of my dad. They started when he was very young, barely more than a baby, but I recognized the dark hair and big green eyes, though I was used to them looking more disappointed. He was on a big red tricycle in one of them, bare feet, bare-chested and muddy. It was a shock. My dad didn't get muddy. He liked to wear nice suits and loafers. This kid in the pictures? He seemed to live in the mud and the outdoors. I hadn't really understood the meaning of flabbergasted until right then.

My grandmother, I decided, looked a lot like me; or, rather, I looked a lot like her. We both had hazel eyes and a tawny pink complexion, but the same could be said of half of the people who claimed their

10

roots in the Appalachia. We had the same ash brown hair, though I kept mine deliberately short. Sure, all the magazines said that most guys liked long hair. That was fine since I wasn't interested in most guys. I wanted a special guy, a particular one; the others could like what they wanted. Besides, when you worked over five fryers, all of them over three hundred degrees, short hair pretty much rocked.

We weren't twins, my grandmother and me. I was shorter than she was, and rounder too, but it was close enough that looking at the pictures gave me the jeebies. It was hard to look at a woman I hadn't known, who looked like me, living a life I had never been a part of. It pretty much sucked.

I left the bookshelves alone and moved on. The kitchen was small, barely more than a single massive sink, a fridge, and a couple of counters. Most of the space was taken up with jars of dried herbs with handwritten labels scrawled over the front. I thought back to the new-age books and decided that my grandma had gone all out with her craft. Good for her. I might not be spiritual, but I was pretty much supportive of people practicing what they liked so long as they didn't force it on me.

The only thing in the fridge and the cupboards was a box of baking soda and a bunch of mismatched dishes.

It wasn't much, I had to admit, but it was more than I had a few weeks ago. It was mine. Or at least it would be after six months here. I wondered why my grandmother had left this all to me. Why not Dad? What had happened between the two of them that was so bad that they couldn't even set it aside when she passed away? These thoughts carried me past the tiny bathroom and to the one and only bedroom.

The bed was a full size, with a massive handmade quilt tossed over the top. There were more shelves here, with even more books and crystals and pieces of materials that I assumed she used for her wind chimes or her craft. In the very center of the bed was a large leather bound book.

Not like the kind that you might get at a kitchy thrift store (I love thrift stores) or anything but the kind that you'd have to order from some fancy company in Italy or something. There was a five-pointed star on the surface, with triangles at each point. The triangles faced different directions, and some of them had lines through the center. I had to admit it was kind of pretty.

I stepped out of my shoes and climbed up on the bed. The mattress was old enough that it sagged comfortably beneath my weight. I tugged the book closer and, out of curiosity, flipped open to the first page. "Liber Magika, a Book of Shadows" was scrawled in fancy writing. I flipped to the next page and read:

"A witch, at all times, is neither good nor evil. The magic she wields simply exists. It is the intention behind her words that matters most."

I frowned at that. I didn't know a whole lot about the New Age movement, but I was pretty sure that there were rules about white and black magic and things like that. Then again, what did I really know? I flipped casually through the first few pages, which I quickly determined was a list of definitions and a picture to go with them. The five-pointed star on the front of the book was a pentacle. Once I read the word, I remembered it. There were a bunch of other terms I didn't really know: athame, which turned out to be some kind of dagger, an esbat, which was sort of like a holy day, and a few others.

"Is this why dad hated you?" I asked to no one in particular. I knew that people who called themselves witches got a lot of hate. Tabitha, a girl I had known very briefly in one of the schools I had gone to, got picked on a lot because she had been Wiccan. I never really understood hating people for what they believed. The world took a lot out of you, why hurt people for what they used to get through it all?

I closed the book and tried not to yawn. I'd been driving all day and all I really wanted was a meal that hadn't been frozen and a good night's sleep. It was already ten o'clock...jeez, how long had I been looking around at things...and the bed was comfortable.

I tugged the heavy quilt around myself and stretched out on one of the five pillows. My eyelids grew instantly heavy. I was in the middle of nodding off when I saw a shape across the street. I was pretty sure it was a guy, but then sleep worked its magic and I didn't think about it anymore.

The sound of my phone going off pulled me out of a dream about a crying woman and floating crystals. I reached blindly for my phone and realized that it was still in my back pocket. I whispered a word of thanks to the gods of technology that I hadn't broken it in my sleep and answered it.

"Hello?"

"Lorena Meredith Quinn, where are you?"

My dad had a talent for making my name into something to be feared. I didn't have that talent. When I use people's full names, I just sound like an idiot.

"Dad?" I asked, even though I knew exactly who it was.

"Where are you?" he repeated.

I could have lied to him. In fact, if I had been more awake, I probably would have. I was not above lying to my dad if it was going to make my life easier, but I needed more than a couple hours of sleep if I am going to do that.

"I'm at Grandma's." I said it defiantly, angrily even. Was I mad at him? Yeah, I really was. I don't know if I had been angry since I got the letter, or if it had started when I realized how alike my grandma and I were, but it had happened.

He went silent, and that's when I knew I was in real trouble. I was nineteen years old. I should be above caring about whether or not I was in trouble with my dad, but it hadn't happened yet. Maybe if I had stayed in school and got that anthropology degree or something I'd feel more like an adult. Yeah. Sure.

"What," he asked, pausing ever so slightly between each word, "are you doing there?"

"Inheriting." I sat up in bed, tugging my feet beneath my body. One of my socks had slipped off while I slept and I decided to dig for it. A quick glance at my phone told me that I had only been out for two hours. "Grandma left her house to me, but I gotta stay here for six months."

"No," he said, as if his word was final.

For a moment, just a moment, I had to resist the urge to do what he told me. My whole life had been doing what my dad said. We had to move somewhere else for his new promotion? I went. He didn't think I should be spending so much time with that guy? I stopped. Plain and simple. I was suddenly really tired of that. Maybe it was the anger. . Maybe it was the lack of sleep. Probably it was both.

"Yeah, so, here's the thing. I'm nineteen now, and if you want me to give up a house and money you are going to have to do better than that."

I was almost surprised. I couldn't remember the last time that I had talked back to my dad. At least not a time when it hadn't been purely in my head or under my breath while behind a closed door. I wasn't scared of my dad, not really. He'd never hit me or anything bad like that, but he had a way of making me feel bad for not following his orders.

"Lorena, it is dangerous for you there. Please come home."

There it was. He sounded sincere. I wanted to believe him, but... "You kept her from me all these years, you even kept her death from me. I'm sorry, Dad, but I'm staying here for now."

"First of all-"

"Sorry, Dad, I need to go. Love you. Bye." I turned off the phone and then switched it to silent. Brave of me, I know, but I didn't need a point by point lecture on why I should be listening to him. He didn't call back right away. I laid back on the pile of pillows, hoping that I'd be able to go right back to sleep. No such luck. With a sigh, I rolled out of the bed, nearly tripped over my own shoes, and stumbled back into the kitchen, hoping for something to eat. No such luck. Whoever had cleaned out my grandma's kitchen had done a really good job.

I pulled out my phone and brought up local late-night restaurants. No luck there either. The only thing anywhere nearby that was still open was a little gas station-convenience store combo. While the idea of prepackaged food wasn't my favorite, I was hungry enough not to care. I queued up my GPS and then got into my trusty powder blue Bug.

The night was cool enough that I had the windows open while I drove through the unfamiliar town. There were all the necessities, all clustered into a trio of shopping centers, but they were outnumbered by a pretty incredible amount of churches. I drove past all of these and parked in the only lot that still had its lights on. A red hatchback took up another spot.

I walked in, a bell chiming over my head, and the girl manning the counter looked up. I guessed that she was close to my age, with high cheekbones and skin in a shade of olive dark enough that I might have called it brown if it weren't for the harsh fluorescent lighting washing her out. Her braids, tipped with more stones, hung nearly to her hips. She wore a smear of blue eye shadow over her amber eyes and a t-shirt that said "Welcome to Night-Vale." She took one look at me and her jaw dropped.

"Grandma!" she called, her voice thick with Appalachia, "You betta come quick. That witch from the prophecy is here."

CHAPTER TWO

There are maybe three or four things that could have been said that might have surprised me more, but I couldn't seem to think of them right then.

"What?" was about all I could manage as I took a single step back towards the door.

The girl behind the counter smiled a billion dollar smile at me. She leaned down and rested her elbows on the countertop so that she could palm her chin between her hands. She had a slew of rings on, all in various precious metals, and a range of stones so wide I couldn't even name but one or two. A necklace slid out of her top, a chunk of clear crystal that reminded me of the collection back at my grandmother's house. "You ain't as scrawny as I thought you'd be."

"Huh?" I looked down at myself. She was right. I wasn't scrawny. I wouldn't call myself fat either, but what did that have to do with anything? Why did she think I'd be anything at all? "What?"

"Might be kinda stupid though."

"Hey!"

"Jenny? What's all this yellin' about?" Another woman stepped out of the backroom. She was older, plump and pleasant to look at. Her hair was every shade of silver and brown and formed a large semi-circle around a face that had the look and texture of carved mahogany. Her shoulders made a perfect line beneath a floral button down shirt. Her dark eyes fell on me and I felt like she could see everything I had ever done. I hoped not, because some of that was embarrassing. "Well now," she said, "what have we here?"

I swallowed hard and put my hand on the door, wishing that my legs would move. The glass was cool beneath my fingers, but I couldn't bring myself to push on it.

"You Ms. Loretta's grandbaby?" the younger girl wanted to know. She brought her hand to the top of her head and patted at the roots of the many braids her dark hair was coiled into.

"No," I said instinctively, remembering only a second later that Loretta was my estranged and now deceased grandmother's name. "Yes. I mean...I think so."

"Well," the girl asked, looking at me like I had grown a set of limbs from an awkward location, "which is it?"

"Hush, Jenny," the older woman admonished. She came around the counter, moving with the kind of speed and grace that you only got if you were really fit. "Come on, then. Let's get a look at you."

She took my chin between two warm fingers that smelled of herbs I couldn't name. Her eyes were big and brown and warm. I couldn't seem to look away, even if I wanted to. Her face had a kindness to it that you could just see, like you could tell her every terrible thing you had ever done and she'd tell you that it was okay. I didn't feel like running anymore, but I was still very confused.

"Yeah," she finally said, turning the single word into twice as many syllables as I would have given it. She dropped her hand from my chin and nodded. "That's her. You look a whole lot like your grandma, you know that?"

I thought back to the pictures I had gone through. I nodded back. "Yes, ma'am."

My father had taught me to say "Ma'am" and "Sir " when the occasion called for it. Four years in customer service had done nothing to help that. She smiled at me, and I knew that her and the girl behind the counter; Jenny, the woman had called her; were definitely related. Both of them had incredible smiles.

"I'm sorry," I said, realizing I could think again, "I don't think you've got the right girl."

"Pshaw," said Jenny, rolling her eyes. Hers weren't brown so much as they were gold, and even from this distance I could see they had a sparkle. "If you Loretta's girl, then you the one from the prophecy, plain and simple."

"Hush, Jenny," the woman said again. She put an arm around my shoulders and guided me deeper into the convenience store. "You gonna scare the girl. Now then, let's try this one again. My name is Marquesa. Most call me Ms. Marquesa or Momma Marquesa; and this is Jenny, my granddaughter."

I did not think the woman was old enough to have a granddaughter, much less one who was old enough to have gone to school with me. I looked between the two of them. The family resemblance was undeniable.

"Hey," Jenny said, her voice thick with the slow speech of Appalachia.

"I'm Lorena," I said, as if they hadn't already figured that one out, "and I am really confused."

"I'm the one that sent you the letter," Ms. Marquesa told me, "I was real good friends with your grandma. We was in the same circle."

"Circle?" I asked.

"Witches," Jenny offered. She made it sound like it was no big deal. Like they had been in the same sewing circle or softball team.

"Oh." I remembered all the crystals and books in my grandmother's house. I had already come to the conclusion that she was into all that new-age stuff. Why I didn't think that she was also in some kind of coven, I don't know.

"I see you gone and figured that much out for your own self," Ms. Marquesa said, "I think that's alright, but you don't know much about the rest, do you?"

I shook my head. "I don't know what you are talking about."

"Well, that's alright. We can fix that up. You hungry?"

I was going to say no out of politeness, but my stomach picked that moment to growl. I blushed. "A little."

"Come on, we got dinner in the back. Let's go sit down. Connie!"

Another girl stuck her head out of the back. She had freckles and a riot of red hair. I could see a series of tattoos peeking out below her olive-green sleeves. "Yeah?" she asked.

"Come watch the front. We gotta go and talk to Loretta's grandbaby," Ms. Marquesa ordered.

Connie gave me a look. It didn't have the same weight as Ms. Marquesa's did, but there was something behind her hazel eyes that made me feel like she was seeing more than just my face. I resisted the urge to cross my arms over myself.

"Yeah, alright then," Connie said. Her voice was so soft that I barely heard it.

Before I knew it, I was being ushered into the employee lounge. There was a whole slew of food. Chicken and seasoned rice and some kind of mixed vegetables in sauce, enough of it to feed a family of five. My mouth watered. I didn't make drooling sounds, but it was a close call.

"Go on, then. Sit down," Jenny pointed to one of the folding chairs. I sat. It was cold against my back.

Ms. Marquesa picked up a plate and started loading it up. I thought she was making it for herself before she shoved it in my direction and took the seat across from me. Jenny stood in the doorway.

"I think I oughta start at the beginning," Marquesa said, "best place after all. I could start with once upon a time or something, but that's best for fables, and this ain't no fable. It's the truth, pure and honest as can be."

"Yeah, it is," Jenny chimed in, moving past her grandmother to pick up dinner for herself.

Remembering that I had my own food, I picked up a plastic fork and took a bite. It was good. Better than good. Maybe it was because I had been living off of fast food recently, but I didn't think so.

"Thank you," I said, indicating the meal.

Ms. Marquesa shook her head. "Think nothin' of it. I know there weren't nothin' to eat at Loretta's place; cleaned it out myself. But anyhow, like I was sayin', once upon a time is for fables, and this isn't one of those. I tell ya that all the things you've read about, faeries and vampires and witches, are all real. Magic is real, it's just sleepin'."

She said it all with that matter of fact tone that another person would have used to describe the weather. I blinked at her, and then at Jenny, and then down at my plate. My mind, being the bastion of witty repartee that it was, could only form one thought: "Wait, what?"

She chuckled. "I could complicate it all, talk about how the world has magic in it, great big roads of it that the average person can't see. I could even give you fancy names like Ley Lines or Magical Weave, or names in a hundred different languages, but the truth is, ya don't really need to know that. What you need to know is that magic used to be strong, but it's grown weak."

"Why?" I asked, feeling intrigued despite myself.

I loved magic. Okay, more accurately, I loved the idea of magic. I liked reading about it, hearing about it, watching movies with it. You name it. Call me a nerd if you want, but I'll just tell you that's a vague and outdated word with no real meaning and keep reading my comic books.

"We don't know," Jenny answered. She shrugged her slender shoulders in an elegant motion and I decided that she wasn't just pretty, she was Cover Girl gorgeous. The blue shadow matched the blue in her jeans and I didn't think it was on accident. "We just know that it stopped working."

"When?"

"Again, we don't know." Jenny pulled apart a piece of chicken and stuffed a good portion of it in her mouth. "But it was a while ago, a couple hundred years, maybe."

"Not that long," Ms. Marquesa interrupted, "but close. Still, we was told it happened because magic needed a rest, it needed to sleep, and so we let it be. Well, most of us, anyhow. Some dabble."

"Witches?"

"Mmmhmm. Witches an' beings that need it to live. But they all went into hiding, pretended to be human while they waited for some sign, something to happen to shake it all up again. They stopped doing the big kind of magics that made everyone believe. They waited for a sign."

"Let me guess," I said, drawing on my years of playing video games, "signs have happened."

"You happened," Jenny said pointedly.

I repeated my super snappy line of, "Wait, what?"

"The prophecy. Didn't your daddy ever tell you why you weren't allowed to come back here?"

I thought about that. I know I had asked, but my dad worked in marketing; he was really good with words and messing with them until they said a whole lot and nothing at all at the same time. Had he ever actually told me why me being with grandma was bad? Aside, of course, from a random late-night phone call no more than thirty minutes ago.

"Just that it was dangerous," I answered, bringing another bite of food to my face.

"Could be, prophecies are fickle things."

There was that word again. Prophecy. I'd read enough fantasy novels to know how those kinds of things ended up. In short? Badly. Prophecies either meant the end of the world or the rising of some great evil and the death of the person they were about. Of all the numerous daydreams that I'd had, I never wanted to be at the center of a prophecy.

"Okay," I said, setting down my half-finished meal, "here's the part where I start to feel confused."

"Your grandma had a gift for seeing things."

"Like looking into the future?" I asked.

Ms. Marquesa nodded her head, reaching up to brush her fingers through her natural curls. "Future, yes, but the present and the past, too. If magic hadn't been sleeping, she'd have been a full-fledged oracle, I believe. Instead, all she got was snapshots, pictures of what had been, and what might be, and a little in between."

There was a sudden sinking feeling in my stomach. I wasn't stupid. Sure, I had dropped out of college before even getting an associate's degree, but that had to do with being lazy, not unintelligent. I could put two and two together. If my dad thought me being here was dangerous, and my grandmother had a gift for prophetic visions or snapshots, and Jenny's first words about me were that I was a witch? Yeah, I saw exactly where this was all going. "And she had a prophetic snapshot? About me?"

"Hole in one, powder puff." Jenny smirked.

"What did she say? What was it about?" That squeaky voice was not me panicking, I swear.

"That you would have the child that brought magic back into the world."

"Oh boy," I managed right before my head went all light and dizzy. I was not going to pass out. Nope. Not going to happen. I swear I was cooler than this. Who was I kidding? No, I wasn't. I was not now, nor had I ever been, anything close to cool. I was on the edge of totally barfing all of that food I had just tossed on an empty stomach.

"Breathe, Lorena," Ms. Marquesa placed a hand on my neck, visible since I had put my forehead between my knees. "It's okay."

"I'm sorry," I said, talking to the denim on my thighs, "I think you and I have really different ideas of what okay means. You just told me I'm going to have a magical prophecy baby. That isn't even in the universe of what I would define as okay."

When I glanced up, all three of them were looking at me, even Connie who was supposed to be watching the front counter. Maybe I got a little louder than I had intended. I was justified. "Are you a witch, too?" I snapped at Connie, feeling a little grumpy.

"Yeah," she answered, as if it were the most normal thing in the world.

"Oh good, then you go give birth to a prophecy." An idea suddenly struck me. "Wait, Jenny said the witch from the prophecy is here. That's not right. It can't be right. I'm not a witch."

The three women exchanged a series of glances that made me feel like I'd said something stupid. I'd like to reiterate that I am not now, nor have I ever been, stupid. I can do stupid things from time to time, but that's not the same thing.

"You are," Ms. Marquesa said gently, moving her hand from the back of my neck to cup my chin. I looked up into her warm eyes and felt just a tiny bit less like throwing up. "You are the granddaughter of one of the most gifted witches ever born on these mountains. You might have swallowed up all of your talent, denied it, but it's there."

"You've got the wrong girl," I protested, "I wouldn't have swallowed anything. Okay? Let me just...let me explain something to you. I wanted to be magical. Okay? I wanted to be someone special when I was a little girl. I wanted to be the girl who turned sixteen and found out she was a witch. I wanted my mom to come back from wherever she had disappeared to and tell me that she was really a goddess and I had inherited her powers.

 If they were looking for kids to try out some cocktail of super drugs in the hopes that they would become better, faster, stronger versions of themselves, I would have been the first one waiving my human rights to give it a go, and eventually throwing on a cape and tight underwear to fight against the undoubtedly evil corporation that spawned me. Okay? I desperately, urgently wanted to be special. But I have not even levitated an object or accidentally cast a spell."

Ms. Marquesa's hand, still a comfortable heat on my skin, gave me the slightest pat. "Oh, Honey, that's not how magic works."

Before she could explain further, an explosion went off. Not the kind that blew stuff up, but the kind that swept down on you, like a hurricane without any wind or rain. It was a change in air pressure, the pounding of someone's overdone amp. All noise without any sound. I clapped my hand over my ears as Jenny and Ms. Marquesa stood up. Connie turned in a tiny circle, throwing her freckled arms wide.

The three of them joined hands, palm to palm. The necklace around Jenny's neck seemed to glow, as did the many rings on her fingers. I was suddenly very aware of that herbal smell emanating from Ms. Marquesa. Connie threw back her head and howled like some kind of wolf. I was pretty sure I heard something answer her.

I wish I could have paid more attention, but the weight of whatever was happening pushed me down to my knees. I pushed harder on my ears but it didn't help. The pressure was sinking into my bones until I thought they would crack.

"Lorena," a woman's voice called. I didn't know it, but it was light and vibrated, "Lorena come to me."

I don't know what I expected to happen. I don't know what I thought I would see when I looked past the trio of women, but I saw a fourth woman in a robe of gray. The hood was so large that I couldn't see her face, but I got the feeling that no one else saw her. They were looking up at the ceiling as if there was something there. Then the image of the woman flickered, skipped like a video that wouldn't stream properly but the sound worked just fine.

"Come to me, Lorena. I'll tell you everything."

I couldn't help myself. I started walking towards her outstretched hands. I wanted to hug her. I wanted to feel her arms wrap around me and make me feel safe. I took one step and then another. My fingers reached out, stretching towards her. I knew if I could just take her hand, everything in the world would be okay. There was a scant inch of space between my hand and hers.

Suddenly, I was jerked backwards, and I found myself staring up into the face of the most attractive man that I had ever seen. Cliché, maybe, but totally true. He had a long sheet of perfectly blond hair, white blonde or platinum. Whatever color you wanted to call it. It was bright. His skin was moonlight pale and his cheeks were sharp as diamonds. He looked like an angel. Not one of those creepy baby ones you saw in those old pictures, or even the alien looking things the Bible actually describes, but a golden-haired angel without the big feathered wings. He swept me into his arms like I was no more than a feather and hugged me to a chest that I was sure had excellent definition. My cheek pillowed against a frilly cravat around his neck, and I realized he wore the outfit of old French Aristocracy.

"No!" the woman cried, but her voice wasn't soft and pretty anymore. It sounded creepy, like a hundred snakes all hissing at the same time. The hand, which had been perfectly formed, now looked withered and ancient and covered in warts. Ew.

The three women let go of one another, throwing their hands to the sky. The pressure suddenly lifted and I could think again.

"Lorena," Jenny called, sounding a little out of breath, "are you alright?"

"I have protected her," the man holding me said.

Being the master of everything suave, I asked, "Who the hell are you?"

"*Ma chère,* I am Alan Pierre Rouergue, of the House of Rouergue, and I am going to be the father of the child that you birth."

CHAPTER THREE

"Yeah," I said, putting my hands on a very attractive chest and pushed, "I'm going to tell you to put me down now. And if you aren't a complete jerk, you are going to listen."

"As you request, *ma chère.*" He put me down, but he didn't exactly move. From my upright position, I could tell he wasn't tall, maybe all of five foot eight or something, but he was all slender lines and elegant features. His nose was a bit sharp and his lips a little thin, but he still would have looked right at home on one of those gothic metal CD covers.

"Personal space, buddy. I don't know you." I gave him a look. I didn't have a mirror, but I was pretty sure it was a meaningful one.

He gave me an amused grin in response and took half a step back. "Oh, but we will, *Cher,* we will. We will make magic together."

His grin blossomed into a full-on smile, and I saw that his teeth, while pearly white, were also sharp and pointed. Nope, definitely not an angel, I decided. I wasn't dumb. I knew vampire teeth when I saw them. These were either the real thing or the best prosthetics I had ever laid eyes on. Considering everything that had happened in the past five minutes, guess which ones I thought they were?

"Right. Apparently, you are supposed to father my prophecy baby."

There were worse options. Okay, that might not be true. For all he was pretty, he could be a level ten mega-creep. But there were probably less attractive options. *Wait? Were there options? Had the prophecy already picked a lover for me?*

I whirled on the three women who were still coming out of whatever weird haze they had thrown themselves into. Their eyes were all still sort of...empty. Ms. Marquesa came out of it first. I wasn't surprised. She seemed to have the most strength. Did strength matter when it came to magic? Maybe. I didn't know. That was pretty much the theme of my life.

"Is he?" I demanded the moment her brown eyes filled with their normal warmth.

"Not...exactly."

"Vague much? Like, dude, I dunno how to tell you this but I am pretty much done with vague. I'm done with just about everything until everyone tells me what the hell that was and who the hell he is and what the hell is going on."

"That was a message," Ms. Marquesa answered.

"Creepy message. Got it. And everything else?"

"We told you there is a prophecy," Jenny answered. With limbs as loose as wet noodles after a five mile run, Jenny flopped into a chair and picked up her not quite finished piece of chicken. When I gave her a look, she gave me an unapologetic shrug. "Magic makes us hungry. It's why we got the good food back here."

Connie gave a silent nod of agreement, but she grabbed a roll from a pile I hadn't noticed before. Apparently, she didn't like to say much.

Ms. Marquesa looked up at me. "The prophecy says that the father of the child will be a vampire from the line of Vlad himself."

"Vlad?" I asked, "As in the Impaler?"

I like history. Sue me. My degree, if I had managed to finish it, would have been in anthropology with a minor in history. I like to study people. They fascinate me. So, when Ms. Marquesa brought up good ol' Vlad, the inspiration for the story of Dracula, I knew exactly who she was talking about. Vlad was a prince of Romania and a heck of a warrior. A lot of history books demonize him for being pretty mean to his enemies, but Romania heralds him as a hero beyond compare. It's all about who writes the story.

"*Oui,* the most brilliant and esteemed prince of blood." Alan bowed his head in respect.

"So...he was really a vampire."

I dragged a hand through my short mop of hair ruining any style that sleeping on it for two hours might have given me. "And Alan is one of his...line."

Alan's lips curled into a smile. He lifted his chin and pushed his nose into the air another inch. "I am."

I was both annoyed by him and amused. It's weird how some people can be both.

"He is but one of three." Ms. Marquesa, who was looking a little gray around the lips, took the chair I had been sitting in. Since there were only two seats, I was left standing. I wasn't bothered. Not only was Ms. Marquesa older than me, this was her place and she had just done some magical stuff to...stop other magical stuff? I was a little unclear about that. "He and his two brothers are...viable applicants for the role."

"Oh," I said dumbly, "cool. Well, I'm not interested."

"What?" All of them said it, in stereo.

"Considering the faces all of you are making, I think you all heard me. I'm not interested in being the oven to your bun of magic. I came here to find out about my grandma and figure some things out about my life. I came here to spend my six months in my grandma's house, get my inheritance and then hit the road. You can see how having a prophecy baby could throw a wrench into the clockwork of my program."

"My, my. She is a snippy little *coquette*, isn't she?"

"Hey, buddy. I know what that word means, and I'm not cool with it. I'm not being a flirt or a tease. I'm laying down the law here. I'm not ready to be anyone's mommy."

There was another series of looks, and I crossed my arms over my chest. They could look at each other all they wanted, but it didn't really matter. I knew what I was going to do.

"I hate to be the bearer of bad news, Lorena, but Loretta was my friend and the stipulations for you receiving her inheritance were...specific."

My world came to a screeching halt. "What?"

"Your grandma made me the executor of her last will and testament. I am in the way of knowin' what it is she said had to happen. Yeah, there is six months of you stayin' at her place. But those months are for you to meet the three brothers and choosing one of them to take as your husband or lover, or what have you."

"What are you saying?" I asked, even though I had pretty much sorted it out of myself. I'm weird. I like to get confirmation that my whole world is about to blow up before I freak out about it.

"I'm saying that you won't get the money until and unless you have a baby."

The pin on the grenade of my future had just been pulled. I could hear it ticking. *Did grenades tick? No. That was bombs. Whatever.*

This had not been the plan. The plan had been simple. Six months here. Get money. Go make a life for myself. But no. That wasn't happening. Instead, a grandma I had never known was telling me what I needed to do with my life and how it needed to be done. I did not approve.

"Are you serious?"

"Yeah," Connie said, breaking her near silence, "she's serious."

30

I dragged my hand through my hair again and tried my best not to just break down and cry. Maybe it had been the sixteen-hour non-stop car ride, maybe it was the shattering of all the dreams I'd had about the temporary house my Dad used to call home, maybe it was the lack of sleep or finding out that magic was very real and I was at the center of the prophecy. Who was I kidding? It was everything and then some. Tears filled my eyes, big and wet and hot.

Jenny gave me a look of compassionate understanding. She stood up and walked around the table. Her arms were warm as she wrapped them around me. "I'm going to get you home."

"Jenny-"

"Grandma, I know a thing or two about life deciding things for ya, let me just...talk to her."

"Wouldn't it be better if-" Alan started.

"No," Jenny interrupted, "it wouldn't. You got some kinda stake in this? Hah, vampire pun. No seriously, you do got your own plan. Right? Right. So back off and give her a few hours to just...soak all of it in, okay fang-boy?"

I let her guide me out of the back room, leaving a trio of quiet people behind us. It felt nice to let her take the driver's seat. She grabbed a bunch of snack treats and candy and guided me out to the car. I let her drive. I wasn't feeling like being at the wheel right that moment. I wasn't even wanting to be in that town right then, maybe not even that state. But what was I going to do?

"Thanks," I said after a couple of minutes of watching unfamiliar street signs pass by. The tears had gone back to whatever emotional pit that spawned them, but I knew they'd come back if I said too much.

"Naw, no worries. Grandma's just excited is all. She sees you coming in and thinks...well...you know what she thinks. I know she

31

might seem overbearing. But she's good. Took me in after mamma and daddy kicked me out for trying to take my girlfriend to prom."

"Are you still dating her?" I asked.

"Naw," Jenny shook her head. "She went off to some fancy college. That's all good. I'll get another girlfriend if I can get off this here damn mountain."

"Not a lot of lesbians around here?" I asked, happy to be discussing a topic that wasn't about me.

"Pshaw, pretty sure Melody and me was the only ones. Tried one of those dating apps once? All the cute lesbians are in Richmond which is like...two hours away and ain't none of them wanna give a chance to some mountain hick."

"That sucks," I said. I meant it. I had dated a girl once. Okay, I had gone on a date with a girl once. It hadn't gone badly, but at the end of it, I realized that I had a preference for guys. Then again, if the right girl found her way into my life, it would not be completely outside the realm of possibility for me to date her. I'm open to options. Oh wait, all the options had been taken from me and narrowed down to three vampire dudes. "I'm sorry."

She shrugged. But I could tell it bothered her. *It had to be hard*, I thought, *to live in a rural town of Virginia if you were not only a lesbian, a black woman, and a witch. Jeez.*

"I'll find someone. Even if I have to fashion her out of magic."

"Well, if I can help, let me know."

"You might, actually," she said, giving me a sidelong glance, "I mean, ain't you Loretta's grandbaby? You got magic in you, too."

I sighed. "See, I said this all right before..."

32

I thought back to the woman in the gray robe, the one with the voice like snakes. I wanted to ask about it, but it felt weird, like it was something I shouldn't be talking about at all. I frowned.

"Before the attack?"

"Yeah," I answered, "what was all that about?"

"Psychic attack," she said, turning onto my street, "probably from the Cult."

She said the word Cult like it ought to be capitalized, like it was important. I pictured the woman in the long gray robes and decided if anyone in my life had ever looked like a cultist, it was her. "Cult, right. That makes perfect sense. Witches, vampires, prophecy. Why not a cult, too? Next thing I need is a brooding stranger and we would officially check off the list of a modern adventure fantasy."

"You haven't met Dmitri yet."

I didn't want to know, but I asked anyway. "Dmitri?"

"One of the other vampires in Vlad's line. Tall, dark and broody." She smirked when she said it. Her eyes twinkling. "If I didn't like women I'd jump him."

"That's a hell of a compliment."

She pulled my car into my grandmother's driveway. "Wait, how are you getting home?" I asked suddenly.

"I'll chill here until Connie gets off of work. She'll pick me up."

I shrugged. "So, we are just going to hang out until then?" I asked.

"If you want. I mean, it's kinda rude to leave the girl who drove you home sitting on ya doorstep, but if that's how you wanna be..."

I rolled my eyes, but smiled anyway. I liked Jenny. Years of moving from one place to another had given me a finely-honed sense of knowing right off who I wanted to hang out with and who I didn't. Jenny fell into the former category. "Come in."

It should have been awkward having someone I didn't know over to a house that wasn't really mine, but like I said, my family moved around a lot. I had become an expert at making friends on the fly. We walked in, unpacked every single packaged and processed food she had taken from the store, and we plopped down in front of my computer to watch cartoons. Because at nineteen, you rediscovered that cartoons were pretty much the best thing ever. Then again, if you are like me, you never forgot in the first place.

"So," she asked, sometime around two in the morning after we had eaten two bags of chips and more Little Debbie snack cakes than I had ever known existed, "tell me what you want to do with your life."

I shrugged. It was hard to think about. "Well, before tonight, my plan consisted of chilling out here for six months and then maybe looking into going back to school in a year or two...you know...after a cruise or a vacation or something."

"Back to school?" She folded her long legs under her and popped open the chip bag that we had promised was going to stay closed forever.

"Yeah, I dropped out earlier this year. I kinda gave up."

"Why?"

I could have lied, but I didn't. "I don't know. I wish I had some great excuse for what I did. I wish I could tell you that I broke under the stress or something...but I didn't. My grades weren't terrible. They weren't fantastic either, but I was managing. The truth, though? I just didn't want to be there anymore. I didn't want to write another paper about the advancement of humans as understood by some random old dude. I didn't want to prove that I know the square root of

34

whatever when I'd been doing that for years already. I thought college was supposed to be different, but as far as I could tell, it was just high school version two-point-oh."

"I wanted to go to college, but we couldn't afford it. An' a'fore you go on and tell me all about the joys of student loans...don't."

I thought back to the couple of thousand that I owed without any degree to show for it. "Not going to happen, I promise. What did you want to study?"

"Geology. I'm good with stones."

"Really?" I asked. I thought back to the psychic attack and remembered the stones glowing around Jenny's throat.

"Yeah, I am. Always have been. Most witches have something they are good with. Well, most have several somethings, but we all have something that we are like...a natural with. The first thing that really bonded with us. I am good with stones, Grandma is good with herbs and kitchen witchery. Connie is good with animals. All of us draw from things. Your Grandma? She was good with metals and the wind."

'Well,' I thought, hearing the tinkle of wind chimes in the distance, *'that made sense.'* If I really was a witch, and I wasn't holding out hope on that front, what would I be good with? I didn't know. I wasn't entirely sure I wanted to find out.

"Who are the vampires?" I asked.

"Well, you met Alan. He's hot."

"And he knows it," I said with a roll of my eyes.

"Oh, ain't that the truth. Yeah, he's nice, but he likes to pretend he ain't. He wears his pretty the way Connie wears her silence."

There was something about the way she said the name that made me look at her. "Do you have a crush on Connie?"

Jenny shrugged her shoulders and looked away. It was clear she didn't want to talk about it. If I had been a best friend, or even a friend for more than two hours, I might have pushed. I didn't though.

"Okay," I said, "you said the other one is named Dmitri?"

"Yeah, he's from Russia, or a place that used to be its own country but is now part of Russia, I dunno. Like I said, he's broody. Tends to act first and think later."

I formed a sketchy picture of him in my head. He ended up looking like that dude who played Aragorn in the Lord of the Rings movies.

"There are three, right?"

She nodded. "Yeah, three. The last one is Wei. I don't know him very well. He's quiet. Really quiet and... intense."

She frowned when she said it, and I frowned right along with her. I could handle quiet guys, and I could handle intense ones, but the guys who were both usually ended up being serial killers. Then again, they were all vampires...

"Do I have to do this?" I asked.

She shook her head. "Naw, you don't have to. But I warn you that prophecy has a way of wanting to be done, even if you don't want it."

"Well I don't. I mean, don't get me wrong. I think it would be cool for magic to be in the world again. Really cool. But...I don't think I want to be the one to do it."

"Well, spend your six months here, do what you gotta do. Maybe get a job and save up. It's all up to you. I'll help out."

She meant it. I could hear it in her voice. It made me smile. "You tryin' to be my friend?"

"There ain't a lot of lesbians on this mountain, but there are even fewer friends."

We shared a quiet moment of complete understanding, the kind between two people who knew exactly what it was like to have a hundred acquaintances and no friends. In that moment, I decided that I'd stick around, if just for Jenny.

There was a knock on the door, and Jenny popped up faster than I could. "That's probably Connie."

I smiled to myself. *Yeah, there was definitely something there. I'd ask about it sometime.* She swung open the door, and I knew that it wasn't Connie, because I heard her ask, "What the hell are y'all doing here?"

"I have informed my brothers of the attack tonight, and we have decided that the vessel of prophecy would be safer at our home than...here."

I recognized Alan's voice. It wasn't just the whisper of a French accent, it was the arrogance in his words. I popped up and stomped over, staring over Jenny's shoulder and right into that perfectly carved face. "Hey, buddy, what did I say about this prophecy thing?"

"I believe you said you were not interested," he said. He was still pretty, and still dressed to the nines in his aristocratic French getup. I had to admit it looked good. Not many guys could pull off that much lace and still look manly. Maybe it was the teeth.

"Y'all need to give her a break. She just got here."

"And already the Cult attacks," a man of maybe twenty or so years old said. He had rich brown hair that curled in natural ringlets around a broad face. His nose was short and hooked, but his lips were soft and looked like they would give excellent kisses. He was also, and I mean this emphatically, buff. Oh, he tried to hide it under loose clothes, so you might not notice at first, but I bet beneath that black shirt and blacker jacket he was built like Mr. Universe.

That had to be Dmitri.

"Well, maybe someone ought to tell them I'm not going to be having any prophecy babies."

Alan gave me a look that said I was being ridiculous. "You will give up your entire inheritance because you do not want to take me as a lover?"

"One of us," Dmitri amended, his voice gruff.

"I'd give up a lot of things to have the freedom that the average woman ought to have, not the least of which is decide when she wants to have a kid," I snapped back.

Alan's lips curled into a smirk. "An independent woman, I see. How...modern."

I rolled my eyes. "Listen, dude, I'm not into this whole alpha male thing. You can take your arrogance and shove it up your pretty-"

"You think I'm pretty?"

If I hadn't already been rolling my eyes, I would have done it again.

"It was just once," Jenny cut in, "They only called to her once. It means nothing. Besides, they attacked at the station. Everyone knows Grandma works her magic outta there. This place is protected. They won't attack her here."

"Yeah," I thought to myself, *"Jenny was definitely going to be my friend."*

"Is that true?" Dmitri demanded.

I opened my mouth to say that it was, but then I remembered the voice I heard when I was just about to drift off. The voice that I had promised myself was nothing.

Jenny turned towards me when my hesitation lasted longer than a second. "Right?"

"Well..."

"She comes with us," a third man said, and all eyes turned towards him. I'd lied. Alan was definitely not the most attractive guy I had ever seen.

Wei, because who the heck else could it be, looked like a modern-day warrior, prepared for battle. A straight-edged blade hung along his back, a tassel hanging off the end. He wore the high neck and straight-sleeved shirt that I associated with Chinese history, but the pants were modern day slacks, loose ones, comfortable enough to move in. The clothes were good, the man in them was devastating. His skin was just a shade or two shy of being gold, with eyes as dark as obsidian. His lips were set into a grim and determined line. He didn't have Alan's elegance or Dmitri's brute strength, but there was something about the way he held himself that told me that this guy took no crap from anyone.

I ignored that completely. "The hell I am."

Jenny gave me a look. "Lorena, maybe you ought to-"

"I don't want to have their children."

I was on the verge of hysterics. I could feel it like a spider crawling up my throat. I shook my head. I knew that if I went with them, I'd be completing some step in this stupid prophecy, and I didn't want that. I wanted to go back to sleep. Better yet, I wanted to not be so stubborn that I quit a job I hated to come looking for a new life.

"Do not be foolish," Wei said, taking a step forward. Everyone moved out of his way, everyone but me. "I have no interest in playing the stud to your brood mare, but you will be safer at our house."

I snorted. "Who the hell called you a stud?"

Jenny made a choking sound that sounded like she was holding back a laugh, Alan's lips spread enough that I could see the tips of his pointed teeth, and Dmitri looked like I had come from a whole other planet. I got the feeling a lot of people didn't stand up to Wei, the Grumpy. Please, I had dealt with Sunday Morning Soccer Moms. No one lays into you like those ladies.

"It was a metaphor."

I shrugged and crossed my arms across my chest. "Nice metaphor since I get to be the brood mare."

His lips made an even tighter line. I put my hand on the door, intending to close it. I don't know what I would have done, because that sense of pressure started to build again.

"Oh no!" Jenny called. She stumbled away from me.

The pressure was hard and fast enough that my ears popped. I knew better than to try and cover my ears, but I did it anyway. Human instinct is stupid that way. The pressure hit me in waves, and I realized it wasn't affecting anyone else, just me. My vision started to go blurry. The men were shouting things to one another, and Wei's arms went around me. I had just enough time to tell him not to get any ideas before I passed out entirely.

CHAPTER FOUR

I woke up in a bed fit for a princess, I kid you not. It had four posters and a canopy and everything. The sheets were the finest cotton I had ever felt, and the comforter was stuffed with feathers. Everything was done in the palest shade of purple. I sat up and tugged at the collar of the nightgown I had not been wearing last night. It was not even a nightgown that I owned.

Come to think of it, I don't think I owned an actual nightgown. Most of my pajamas were one of three pairs of sweat pants and an appropriately geeky t-shirt. I did have a Wonder Woman matched set, but that's not what I was wearing now. This was frilly and flowy and girly. Not something I would have picked out for myself.

I wondered who had changed my clothes, and then decided that I didn't want to know.

The afternoon sun spilled in through a window that might have looked more at home in a church than a bedroom. It had stained glass cut into shapes to look like a massive rose garden. It took me a moment to realize that it wasn't just a window; it was a door, and beyond that was a little balcony. I didn't go out there, but I could see the shadow of it. I'd never stayed in a place nice enough to have stained glass anything.

I swung my feet out and instantly regretted it. It was cold! I guess vampires didn't need much in the way of heat, and I was currently assuming that in my knocked-out state, I had lost the argument about where I would be staying. Either that or the Cult had gotten me. That would be a neat twist. I looked around and found a pair of slippers and a robe. I tugged both on and got a look at myself in the mirror of a cute vanity tucked carefully into one corner of a room large enough to fit most of the apartments I had grown up in.

My short hair was sticking up in a hundred places, and my eyes had the kind of bags that would have to be checked at the airport, but other than that, I looked okay. It could have been worse.

I opened a closet and the drawers to the standing dresser. I found not only the few clothes that I had brought with me, but twenty or thirty outfits that were definitely not my style. Too many lacy bits. I wasn't above wearing a dress. I liked dresses, but lace itched, and bows were for little girls. I didn't change, mostly because it was cold and I had no desire to take off the robe that had begun to warm me up. Instead, I decided to go investigating.

I liked anthropology. Okay, there were four different types of anthropology. Thanks to the slew of crime shows on television, most people were aware of forensic anthropology, the study of bones and such. I studied social anthropology, which means I looked at pots that had been in some thousand-year-old dump site and tried to determine what they meant to someone. It was sort of like archaeology; they went hand in hand. Even so, my year and half of taking classes had given me insight into people based off of the things that they kept around. Whoever had decorated this room liked things to be comfortable and attractive. I was okay with that.

I opened the door and peeked out. No one was there. A long red rug bisected a hallway built of dark wood. There were sconces every few feet and doors on either side, five doors if I was counting right. I walked past them and towards a massive staircase. There were stairs leading up and down, which made it difficult to figure out what floor I was on.

"Miss?"

I nearly jumped out of my skin. I whirled and found myself facing a very tall, very slender, very bald man.

"I did not mean to startle you."

"Then wear a bell!" I said pressing my hand to my chest. My heart was going a billion miles an hour. "And be glad I am not a ninja."

His lips moved up into a shadow of a smile. "As you wish."

"Who are you?"

The man bowed in my direction, placing one hand at his chest. "My name is Peter Montague and I am the butler here."

Of course, there would be a butler. I don't know why I hadn't thought it before. Pretty stained glass, frilly clothes, and domestic servants. They were like peas in the pod of privilege. Neat.

"Hi, Pete," I said, keeping my robe closed. While the nightgown I wore went from neck to floor, the fabric was pretty thin. "I'm Lorena."

"So, I was informed. I wish to convey my apologies for your treatment. The young masters of the house do not usually bring home unconscious women against their will."

"Well, they've done it often enough to piss me off," I shot back, then felt bad about it. Peter wasn't the one who had brought me here. He was just apologizing for it. "Sorry. Who told you I didn't want to come?"

"Miss Jenny did. She asked me to give you this."

He held up one hand. How I hadn't noticed my grandmother's book of magic before I wasn't sure. Then again, the hall wasn't well lit, and I was feeling out of my element. There was a post-it note on the front. It had a phone number on it.

"Call me when you wake up." A large 'J' was written in stark handwriting at the bottom.

"Thanks."

"Are you hungry?" he asked.

"What time is it?"

"Nearly four-thirty. The gentlemen will be abed for a few more hours. I thought you might like some time to yourself before they wake. I do not expect that they will give you much in the way of peace."

I agreed with Pete there. I was pretty sure once the boys were awake, I was going to be beset with questions, made demands of, and probably wooed. Or at least attempts at being wooed. I wasn't feeling very woo-able right this moment.

"Breakfast would be good. Um...is there a shower?"

"Your room has an en-suite."

"I... have no idea what that is, but I'm pretty sure I would have found it."

He smiled at me, and I could tell I had amused him. I wasn't sure how. He moved past me and opened the door to my room. If he noticed all the doors hanging open and drawers half pulled out, he didn't say anything. He went to one side of the dresser and pushed a button I hadn't seen before. What looked like another part of the wall swung open to reveal the kind of bathroom you expected to find in a castle. Then again, maybe we were in a castle. I didn't know.

"Wow," I said, eyeing the bathtub that could have fit three of me comfortably.

"Indeed. I shall prepare something for you. Do you have any dietary restrictions I should be aware of?"

"I'm allergic to tree nuts," I said, "I have an epi-pen in my purse just in... Wait, where is the box?"

"The box?" he asked.

"Yes, the box. My box of personal things."

"The box was placed in the library as most of the items were books. Would you prefer that it be brought up here?"

"Yes, please."

He bowed his head. "I shall see to it. Take your time. Food will be prepared when you are."

He left as quietly as he had snuck up on me. I wondered if he was human. He looked pretty human to me. Were magical people allowed to be bald? I don't think I had ever seen one that was. Then again, that had always been on television, and TV didn't seem to like bald people either.

I took longer in the bath than I should have, but it felt so good. There were ten different bath soaps and four jars of those beads that made the water feel silky. I tried a combination of stuff and sank into water than smelled like springtime and just sat there. Besides, it gave me time to think.

So, I was the girl from the prophecy. I was supposed to take a vampire lover and give birth to a child who would wake magic up. I was also, apparently, a witch. If I was being completely honest with myself, I liked the idea of all of the above.

 I liked the idea of being a witch, of having a vampire boyfriend and a baby who was, from birth, special. But I didn't like all of these things being forced on me. I was tired of that. My dad had done that all my life. I certainly didn't want my adult life starting off the same way. I was just going to have to calmly explain that to the vampires.

And then what? Go back to my grandmother's house where I had been attacked by strange magic I didn't know and things I couldn't fight? No, thank you. So what was I going to do? I used some fancy shampoo that smelled like fruit in my hair as I thought it over.

I'd need to learn how to defend myself. I was not an athlete. I wasn't out of shape or anything, but I had always elected to walk a mile rather than run it. I was a bit on the busty side and even the best sports bras didn't stop the pain of the jiggle that came with running, jumping, and other forms of sports. I preferred my feats of strength to be done digitally.

I looked at my grandmother's book, which I had left sitting on the toilet lid. I could learn magic. If I was supposed to be a witch, then shouldn't I at least try to learn? Yeah, I knew that this also sealed the deal on my being prophecy-mom, but that didn't mean I didn't want to learn of my own accord.

So long as I didn't take a vampire on a ride, I should be perfectly okay, right? Right.

Okay, so that was decided. I would learn magic. Cool. I'd call Jenny and talk to her about that after I got something to eat. I rinsed my hair and unplugged the tub. By the time I was dressed in my own clothes, a pair of skin-tight jeans and a Captain America shirt, all I had to do to find the kitchen was follow the heavenly scent of smells coming out of it. There was a massive table in the dining room, but a smaller table in the kitchen. I took the smaller one and watched Peter work.

"Hello, Miss," he said cheerfully.

"Hey, Pete, what's on the menu?"

"Eggs Benedict with a side of fruit and tea."

"Yum," I said. I meant it. I was halfway through my breakfast when another door opened. Peter glanced past me.

"You are awake." Dmitri's voice was even more ragged now than it had been yesterday. Apparently, he did not wake up easily. I turned and discovered that I was right. He looked like a tousled bear, his curly hair all around his face. He wore a pair of loose pajama bottoms and nothing else. I was right; he was buff. Really buff. He had washboard abs and defined pecs and everything. There was a tattoo on one shoulder; it was old and simple, a series of interconnected lines and dots that I could make a picture of. "I had hoped to be up before you."

"Why?" I wanted to know, sipping at my cooled-off tea.

"I had..." he shrugged, letting his voice trail off, "It does not matter. You are here now, and here you shall stay."

"Master Dmitri, forgive my saying so, but that is hardly the way to talk to a young lady."

Dmitri growled. "She is being difficult about the prophecy."

"*She,*" I said, pushing the rest of my food away, "is right here and she just wants to make her own life choices, thank you very much."

"Ah, are we breaking our fast together this morning?"

Alan seemed to appear out of nowhere. No, seriously. One moment he wasn't there, the next he was. Unlike Dmitri, he looked as fresh as a daisy, or whatever the saying was. He wore a pair of expensive pajamas in deep red silk. Usually people that pale, like me, couldn't get away with wearing red. It brought out the flush in our cheeks or the random red patches of skin, but he managed it well. The first two buttons of his top were undone, showing the perfect marble of his chest beneath.

"Good morning, *ma cher*," he said, taking my hand and kissing the back of the knuckles, "I trust you slept well."

"Well enough," I answered, "Do vampires sleep?"

"We...rest," Dmitri answered. He slid into one of the other chairs at the small table and poured himself a glass of juice.

"Wait, don't vampires drink blood?"

"So?" Dmitri asked, "That doesn't mean we don't like to taste other things."

47

"How does the blood drinking work?" I wanted to know.

Alan's arm slid around my middle, I found myself scooped towards him as if we were dancing, his eyes, bright as rubies, glittered down at me. I felt a mixture of interest and uncertainty rush through me. My heartbeat jumped right up into my throat.

"I could show you," he whispered.

I opened my mouth to tell him to back up, but I never got the chance. There was a flurry of movement, and the next thing I knew, I was on the ground and Dmitri was holding Alan against the wall, his hands around the other man's throat, as he shouted something in a language that I was guessing was Russian. The very nice painting behind them was ripped in three places as Alan scrambled to fight back.

Dmitri, I could tell, was the stronger of the two, but Alan was slick. Claws formed where once there had been oval fingernails, and he swept at the larger male. Dmitri relented just enough to allow Alan the space he needed to push away from the wall. Peter put one hand on my shoulder and drew me away from the fight.

Without the wall to keep them in place, they moved with a speed I could barely follow. They were a blur of dark clothes and darker clothes that rolled over one another, one spouting French and the other Russian. I didn't know either language. I had taken German in high school and American Sign Language in college, but I was pretty sure that none of the words were pleasant.

"Are they fighting over me?" I asked.

"It would seem so," Peter answered.

I rolled my eyes. Some girls wanted a bunch of guys to fight over them. More power to those chicks, may they see the most epic of battles. That wasn't me. I just wanted one guy. Just one who liked the things that I liked and thought I was awesome. Was that so much to ask?

'Yes,' I thought as Dmitri dropped Alan through a table, 'apparently it was.'

"Stop it!" I shouted. No one listened. "Hey! Stop it."

I didn't even see Wei coming. Like Alan, he just seemed to appear out of nothingness. He wore a robe, belted around his middle, and nothing else. I got a pretty good glimpse of thigh as he pulled the other two apart. I might have appreciated it more if he held up both men at the same time as if they were nothing but misbehaving children. His long hair came out of the coiled style it had been in and fell around him like a sheet of night. I swallowed and took a step back. I might be offended, but I was also intimidated.

"You will cease this stupidity." Wei's voice was completely and totally calm.

"He-"

"No." Wei interrupted whatever Dmitri had been about to say. He looked between the two of them. "You both wish to be accepted by the witch, and yet you behave like idiots."

It was true, but he didn't have to say it like that.

"It was...my fault," Alan admitted, "Lorena showed interest in understanding the intricacies of blood feeding and I took a chance."

"Did you feed on her?" Wei asked. The way he said it made me think that the answer would be very important.

"No, Dmitri...intervened."

"Okay," I said, finding my voice, "Does someone want to explain to me why this was a big deal?"

Wei dropped the two men. He gave me a look that let me know he thought very little of me for not already knowing. "You are not aware of the power that a vampire's bite can have?"

"Nope," I said, refusing to be ashamed. Until last night, I hadn't even known that vampires were a real thing. I wasn't going to feel bad for not knowing everything a few hours later.

He narrowed his dark eyes at me. "Stupid."

I might have waived him off, but he had just gone all Superman on the other vampires. I didn't feel like testing those waters. "Rather than call me names, how about you educate me?"

"It is not my job to relieve you of your stupidity."

"If you aren't willing to bother, then don't be surprised when I don't know something."

He frowned at me as if I had finally said something interesting. I don't know what it was, but I was just happy he wasn't being a jerk anymore.

"The bite from a vampire can be hypnotic," Alan finally said, "It is...intoxicating. If done well, and over a period of time, a human can become enamored of it."

"So, it's like a roofie."

"A poor comparison, but not without merit," Alan bowed, "Forgive me, I lost my senses for a moment. While the bite is intoxicating to humans, for us it is...maddening."

"Oh," I said feeling as stupid as Wei seemed to think I was, "good."

"We should discuss these things," Dmitri said, rubbing the back of his neck, "and others,"

"Shall we have breakfast?" Alan asked, trying to look cheerful.

"What is there to discuss?" I wanted to know. I was serious. What exactly did they want to talk about, because I was getting the distinct impression I wasn't going to like what was being said. Heck, so far nothing that I had heard made me feel any better about anything.

I didn't say anything, but I took my seat in front of a breakfast that had long since gone cold. I frowned at it. I hate cold eggs. Peter, who seemed to understand my predicament, picked up the plate. His long-fingered hand wove over the top, and when he set it back down, my breakfast was as good as new.

Definitely not human.

"The first thing we need to discuss," Alan said, taking the seat on my right, "is what we are going to do about Lorena."

"Lorena has decided that you guys aren't going to do anything about her," I said, cutting into my eggs. "She has also decided that she isn't impressed with the way you keep talking about her rather than to her."

"Women were not so...outspoken...when I was alive," Dmitri said.

"Welcome to the twenty-first century."

"They were plenty outspoken when I was alive," Alan put in, "wildly so."

"Good for them," I shot back, "But what is it you guys need to decide?"

"We need to keep these fights from happening. I will not always be here to break them apart," Wei said. He hadn't sat down. Instead, he stood there with his arms across his chest.

"How about they get it through their thick skulls that I have no interest in being with any of you?" I asked.

"That is not true," Alan retorted, "I felt the way you shivered when I held you. And, while I do not like to admit it, I saw the way you looking at the impressive chest of Dmitri, and if I am not mistaken, you are even impressed by our implacable Master Wei."

I blushed. I didn't want to admit it, but they were all very attractive men. Yes, they were all different, but attractive. I'd have to be blind not to see that. And yeah, if I was being honest, I was a little flattered that they were all vying for my attention, but that didn't make it okay.

"I'm human," I said by way of defense.

"Indeed." Wei's nose crinkled in disgust.

"Grow up," I snapped, "So what if I think you guys are all hot? I know the difference between 'ooo pretty' and 'I want to go to bed with you'."

"I request that you give us a chance," Alan offered, "All of us."

"What?" I asked. Queen of the snappy replies, that's me.

"We would like to court you, date you if you will."

"All of you?"

"Not me," Wei supplied. I had pretty much figured that out.

"If Wei wishes to be as foolish as he proclaims everyone is, that is entirely his decision. But for myself and Dmitri, I request that you allow us both time with you to show you that while there is a prophecy involved, you may enjoy our company in spite of it, not because of it."

It was carefully phrased, worded just enough that I felt like I had a choice in this. "And if I don't? Will you just throw me to this Cult?"

He sighed, placing his hand over his heart as if I struck him. "I would never let a woman be hurt simply because she does not find my company charming."

"Me either," Dmitri grumbled.

"Okay," I said. I don't know who was more surprised, them or me. I hadn't even realized that I was going to agree until the word was out of my mouth. So I'd go out on a few dates with a couple of super-hot vampires. So what? I'd have fun, and when the time came to move on, I would. Dating did not equal sleeping with.

"Really?" Dmitri asked.

"Why?" Wei demanded.

I said the first thing that came to my mind. "I'm young. They are hot. I've never had the chance to have one boyfriend let alone two. Besides, what do you care? You have no interest in me anyway."

His lip curled up in a sneer as I pushed my now empty plate away. "We can start tomorrow. Alan gets first date."

"Why?" This time it was Dmitri demanding.

"Because his name starts with an A," I answered, pulling my phone out of my pocket. I sent Jenny a text letting her know I was awake and ready to learn some magic. Her response was a couple of confetti emojis. I was going to take that as a good thing.

"Where are you going?" Wei wanted to know as I pushed past them.

"To learn magic."

CHAPTER FIVE

The red hatchback that I had spotted in the parking lot the night before carried Jenny, Connie, and myself back to the house my grandmother had left me.

"Why there?" I asked when Jenny had told me where we were going.

"Because, it's got books and wards."

"The wards didn't keep us safe last night," I said, passingly familiar with the idea that a ward was supposed to protect things.

"Naw," Connie said, "but it'll keep us from blowing up."

Well, I thought, that was good enough for me. Besides, after deciding that I'd date both Dmitri and Alan, I needed to get out of the house. Just saying it had changed the way everything felt. Alan and Dmitri both looked at me as if I was...available. Wei did not. Neither did Peter, come to think of it.

Jenny pulled her hatchback into the parking spot and we all piled out. It was a nice night, colder than the one before, but the moon and the stars were out. The three of us headed in, and I felt a rush of guilt for having left the place so messy. The bags of candies and chips were still cluttered everywhere, mixing with the more organized clutter of my grandmother's home.

"So," I said after I apologized thirty times and picked everything up, "what do we do?"

"Did you bring the book?" Connie asked. She was wearing a hoodie today, done in pink camo. Her jeans were torn in several places.

I looked at my purse, which was barely large enough to fit a paperback much less my grandmother's great big magic book. "Uhhh, no."

"It's fine," Jenny said, waving a ring-bedecked hand. She was wearing a denim blouse today, and a pair of dark slacks that clung to her legs. "We just need to go over the basics. We don't need a book for that."

She knelt on the ground, and Connie and I did, too. The three of us formed a triangle, and I was reminded of the triangles that surrounded the pentacle on my grandmother's book.

"The only thing that separates a witch from a regular person is her ability to tap into the Weave," Jenny explained, "Grandma told' ja about the Weave last night."

I had a vague recollection. "The...um...the lines of magic?" I guessed.

"That's them. It's kinda like a big invisible grid stretched out over the whole world, but it's not a perfect one. In some places, the lines are close together, in some they are small, and others they're thick. When you stand on one, it's easier to do magic. If you stand at a crossroads, a place where two touch, it's even easier."

"Can anyone be a witch? Or do you have to be born one?"

"Don't matter. Grandma didn't look into witchcraft until after Paw-Paw died. Ms. Loretta helped her out there. Said that my grandma had a gift for it, even though she weren't born to it. I know it's easier if it's in your family...but not because of any hereditary talent...mostly because you just know about it growing up, I guess. Connie don't have any magic in her background."

"Nope," Connie agreed.

"Okay," I said, pretty sure I understood, "So why the stones? Or the metal?" I asked.

"Makes it easier," Connie said.

"Yeah," Jenny agreed, "it sure do. Like...think of it like painting or something. You can do a fine sketch if you got a piece of paper and your number two pencil, right? But if you got the desk, the chair, the good paper and all the fancy pencils...you can do more. It doesn't mean that the art's gonna be much bettah' but it sure do help."

That made sense to me. "Okay," I said, "so your stones are like your...favorite medium."

Jenny's face lit up like a firework. "Exactly! They are what works best for me, my style or whatever. Connie here is good with animals, dogs especially. Says it's because she basically a dog."

"Am not," Connie said with a smirk. She flopped back and flicked a hand across her ear as if she were a mutt scratching at her face.

"Are too," Jenny teased back.

The girls giggled. After a moment, I did, too. Connie threw her head back and howled. A wolf somewhere on the mountain answered.

"See, if Connie wanted to, she could call a whole pack of dogs, and a lot of other critters to come and help her."

"So, Connie's a Disney princess?"

It was Connie's turn to blush. "Phsaw." She waved one hand, but I could tell she was pleased. I wondered if anyone called Connie a princess often or just recognized her as a girl. Both times I had seen her, she wore big clothes. Her riot of red hair was neither short nor long. She didn't wear make-up, and her boots were heavy. She looked, in my opinion, androgynous. Maybe that was the style she wanted. That was her choice.

"Hah!" Jenny let out a bark of laughter that dissolved into a series of whoops. "Oh yes, Disney princess, that's her alright."

"Shut up," Connie said, but she was smiling.

"So, we gotta figure out what you good with," Jenny said, "and that can take a lot of time."

"How will I know what I'm good at?" I asked.

"You'll know," Connie answered.
"Yeah, you'll just...know. Some people say it's a warmth, others say it's a tingle. But once you recognize it...you just know," added Jenny.

It sounded vague to me, but I was willing to give it a go.
"Okay...how do I start?"

"Well, we are going to set out a bunch of objects, and you are going to try to summon the spirit out of them."

"I'm going to do what now?" I asked, feeling like she had suddenly slipped into a different language.

"All things, man-made or natural, got spirit. Like...you ever touch something and it give you a chill, but you don't know why? Or just felt the urge to put your hand on a tree?"

I thought about it. "Yeah, I guess so," I said, even though I wasn't completely positive.

"It's like that."

The girls laid out a bunch of what they called "the regulars." A small mirror, a candle, a cup of water, a match, a couple of herbs, and a few others.

"So, summoning the spirit of something is just like this." Jenny held her hand out over a rock. I didn't see anything. Nothing glowed or sparkled. The stone didn't leap to her hand, but there was an...energy. Like a hearty breeze without the wind.

"Is that...spirit?" I asked.

"Yup," Jenny beamed.

"What...what's the point of it?" I wanted to know. "How does that...help?"

"Witches are about gettin' things to respond to them. They sort of...tug at magic to change the world. I could ask this here spirit if it will keep me from being hungry. It might bring me a pizza or, more likely, it'll plant me a garden that I have to take care of. Earthy things, like rocks, aren't big into the 'here and now' they are more about the long term."

"Couldn't you be specific?" I asked.

Connie shook her head emphatically. "No. That's bad."

"Why?" I wanted to know.

"Spirits don't like being told what to do...they like to be asked." Jenny patted the top of her braids.

Okay, while it sounded weird, I could totally understand that. I liked being asked, too. It was sort of my big issue with life.

"Okay," I said, holding my hand over the mirror, "let's do this."

"Picture the item coming alive beneath your palm. Ask it to."

I tried. I really did. I tried so hard my hand shook. Nothing happened other than a really annoying hand cramp.

"Not a mirror witch," Connie said.

"Pro'ly for the best. Mirror witches can get really vain."

"So, you change once you find the...medium?" I asked.

Connie shrugged. Jenny frowned.

"Sorta? Like...your personality and your medium kinda...match. You don't much change, but after it happens everything sorta clicks for you."

"Okay," I moved on to the candle, and then the match. An hour later, I had tested twenty objects and was no closer to clicking with any of them. All I had was a massive headache.

"It's okay," Jenny said for the fifth time in as many minutes, "your grandma didn't know at first either."

I wasn't sure if I was comforted by that or not. "How about you just teach me some more?"

They did. Jenny and Connie alternated between passing off bits and pieces of information that they knew, and I used my phone to save the notes. Who said a book of magic couldn't be digital? I learned that there were five basic European elements, but those elements were different once you got to countries that spoke Mandarin; Earth, Air, Fire, and Water. The four of them combined to make Spirit, which was said to be the most powerful element.

It was not to be confused with spirits, which were usually associated with one of the four lesser elements. Witches could, once they woke up all that magic inside them, contact spirits and seek boons from them. Usually, they had to sacrifice something. Not a baby or anything terrible, but like...a piece of cake or a bit of jewelry or something.

Two hours after that, Jenny threw in the towel. She pulled a few books off the shelves and told me I ought to read them over the next few days. *Oh goodie. I had homework.* I was pretty much terrible at homework. There were always far more interesting things to do when I got home...like cleaning out my hairbrush or mowing the lawn. Laziness might not be the only reason I had dropped out of college.

"It's late, how bout we go to the drive-in?" she asked, now that homework had been assigned.

I sprang up, my legs quaking from having been in the same position for too long. "There's a drive-in? Like, an honest to god drive-in?"

Connie snorted. "One of the last ones left in America."

"Oh, we are so totally going. I don't care what's playing. We are going."

We piled into the hatchback. Jenny determined it was just cool enough that she could take off the top of her car, revealing that it had a T-shaped roof. It felt good, no it felt great, to drive around the mountain with the two of them, giggling as the wind did terrible things to our hair and heading towards the drive-in. We got popcorn and massive sodas, then settled in to watch the double feature for a couple of black and white horror flicks.

"Ooo!" Connie adjusted her seat so that it was nearly laid back. She folded her hands across her stomach, and the sleeves of her shirt slid up enough that I could see tattoos. "I like this one!"

"Oooo!" I said, reaching for her arm. "I like those. Can I see?"

She thrust her arm in my general direction, which I took to mean I could ogle. I loved tattoos. I didn't have any of my own. I was too poor and just a tad jittery at the idea of volunteering my flesh for needlework, but I loved the way they looked.

The tattoos on the inner arm of her otherwise freckled skin were, so far as I could tell, symbolic. Not the usual flowers or Celtic animals or butterflies that I was used to seeing girls get (no shame, by the way; pretty floral tattoos were nothing but win), but these were all hard geometric shapes layered on top of one another until they formed strange patterns that were hard for my eyes to follow.

"Neat," I said with honest enthusiasm. "What do they mean?"

"Protection," Connie answered in her usual succinct self.

I glanced over to Jenny for further explanation.

"Our biggest enemy is corruption magic," Jenny said, her own eyes following the inky patterns on Connie's skin. "It.well, corrupts the very world around it. The rumor is, even though we can't prove it, that corruption is what helped magic fail."

"Oh," I answered, my brows drawing together. "Why can't we prove it?"

Connie snorted. "Because it's all magic."

I didn't understand exactly what that meant, but Jenny seemed okay with the answer. Besides, the movie was past the credits now and was getting into plot. I tossed my legs over the center console, and Jenny curled up in her seat like a cat.

Somewhere in between creature-feature one and creature-feature two, I realized that I had made not one, but two friends in twenty-four hours. It was not a bad way to start a brand-new life as a witch.

CHAPTER SIX

"Where have you been?" Wei demanded the moment that Jenny dropped me off back at home. He stood in the archway between the foyer and the rest of the house like some kind of moody sentinel. He wore silk from neck to ankle, the kind of outfit you might have seen in some historically inaccurate depiction of a Chinese monk, all in deep reds. The red brought out all those golden undertones in his tawny skin. His long dark hair was coiled into a braid as thick around as my arm. He would have been grade A hot if it weren't for the seriously grumpy expression on his face.

The good feelings that I had been fostering thanks to my time out with new friends evaporated. There was pretty much nothing I hated more than having my happy feelings ruined by someone else's crappy mood. There was a reason I didn't work out in fast food...or college.

"Out," I snapped back, "What do you care?"

"We could not contact you."

"My phone was off." I tried to walk past him, but for a guy who was pretty much a scant inch taller than I, he managed to take up a lot of space. Maybe it was the shoulders. They were pretty wide and defined. I couldn't help but notice since his silky shirt didn't have any sleeves.

His eyes managed to be dark and bright all at the same time as he glared at me. "You are no longer allowed to do that."

"Excuse me?" I planted my palms on my hips and squared my own, somewhat less substantial, shoulders. "You are not my father and, hell, I didn't even listen half the time he told me to do something."

Okay, that wasn't true. Until yesterday morning, I almost always listened to my dad. I wasn't proud of that. I'd have probably been a lot better at being an adult if I had rebelled from time to time, but Wei didn't need to know that.

His lips thinned into a disapproving line. "You do not honor your parents?"

I rolled my eyes so hard I nearly saw my brain. "Dude, my mom hightailed it out of my life before I was blowing spit bubbles, and my dad has done nothing but lie to me about the how's and why's of his decision to keep me away from this part of my life. As far as I'm concerned, they aren't worthy of honor."

I found I was able to shove past him, but I think it was just because he was too shocked by my words to remember he was blocking me from heading upstairs. I tried to ignore the tingle on my arm where it brushed his. Why were grumpy guys so hot? Seemed kinda counter-intuitive to a happy relationship.

I hadn't gotten too far when I ran headlong into Dmitri. He hadn't bothered with a shirt at all. He held a rag between his hands and was scrubbing flecks of paint from his skin. His jeans rode low enough on his hips to show off a very masculine V of musculature. Hell, there was nothing but muscles on him. A smear of blue paint decorated the broad expanse of his chest. I wondered if he had been half dressed on purpose, or if he usually painted half naked. I guess it would save him a lot of ruined clothes.

"You got something to say, too?" I demanded.

He held up one large hand in a show of surrender. The other waved the white cloth like a flag. "It is not my place to tell you what you should be doing with your life, Lorena."

With the rich Russian accent, he managed to turn my name into something exotic. I kinda liked it. "You are damn right it isn't."

He dipped his head in apology. Was this the same vampire boy who had gone all feral and attacked Alan? He certainly wasn't acting like an animal now.

"Your life is yours to do with what you please, but I ask you to remember that your actions affect those around you. We were worried."

"Why?" I demanded, partially because I was still riding the anger train, and partially because his words started a wave of guilt. "Because you guys couldn't spend your time wooing me?"

He shrugged his shoulders, and his chest became a distracting display of movement. Jeez, did he bench press cars? His dark hair fell over his face, and he reached up to push it out of his eyes.

"I will not lie to you, Lorena, the opportunity to win your attention is a hard temptation to ignore. It is one we do not often get."

"Why?" I wanted to know. It had been my favorite question this week. Heck, it had been my favorite question since I was two. "None of you have any vampire girlfriends to choose from?"

He frowned at me. "There aren't very many vampires in general, and even fewer female ones."

"Why?" I asked again.

"The process to become one of us is both lengthy and painful. It pushes a body to the very limits of pain," he answered.

"You think women can't take pain?"

His lip quirked up in a grin that I would have called boyish were it not for the hint of fang that it exposed. "I am not so foolish as to think such a thing. I cannot answer for all women, but I can say that one cannot become a vampire against their will. It is something that must be chosen, and I think women are wiser to decide that the price for eternal life is not worth it."

"You're a poet," I said suddenly.

He blushed. Really blushed. It was quite possibly the cutest thing I had ever seen. His nearly boyish grin turned sheepish, and he dragged his paint flecked fingers through his dark hair, leaving behind a few flecks of white and blue in the dark locks.

"I have...dabbled."

"Can I see?" I asked.

He looked up at me. His eyes sparkled with something I might have called hope. "You enjoy reading?"

I leaned one hip against a large heavy chair, crossing one foot over the other. "I moved around a lot as a kid. I never had a problem making friends. I'm sociable or whatever, but it was hard to feel close to anyone when I knew I was just going to leave again. But books? I could always count on books."

"Have you seen the library?"

"You guys have a library?"

I don't know why I hadn't already assumed that this big old house would have a haven of books, but it literally had not entered my head. I hadn't seen a television anywhere, so I don't know what else I expected creatures of the night to do with their free time. I was pretty sure that they didn't have jobs.

"I could...show you?"

It was an offer, not a demand, and that meant a lot to me. I looked at my phone. It was late, really late, and I was tired, but the lure of books was pretty intense for a bibliophile like myself. "Alright, but I'll need to get to bed soon."

He offered me his arm like he was some kind of knight. Maybe he was. Did Russia had knights, long ago? I didn't know, but I should probably find out. Heck, I should probably learn about all these guys. While I still had no intention of carrying some magic baby, I wasn't completely immune to the idea of being wooed by three really attractive men. Okay, two really attractive men. Wei had made it very clear that he was in no way interested.

"Does Wei hate me?" I asked as I curled my fingers over a very impressive bicep.

"Wei doesn't hate anything," Dmitri promised, "but he doesn't like being told what to do."

I couldn't blame him for that, but I wasn't sure that there wasn't some animosity there. I didn't push on that, though. It felt weird to ask one guy too much about another. I might not have had any actual boyfriends in my life, but I wasn't completely without knowledge. Thanks, Cosmo.

Now that I wasn't completely exhausted or barely awake, I got to see the house in all of its late-night glory. It was half museum, half historical movie backdrop. There were incredible paintings along the walls, some of people and some of places. I glanced at the smear of blue, now at eye level, and then at the paintings. "Are these yours?"

He blushed again. Man, it was really cute when he did that.

"They are."

"Poetry, painting, what else do you do?"

"I used to ride horses," he admitted.

"Horses?" I asked. It was far too easy to imagine him on horseback with some kind of weapon in his hand.

"My people lived a great deal of their time on horseback. I was on a horse before I had seen three winters. I had my own horse to take care of."

"Where did you live?" I asked as he led me down the labyrinth of halls.

"It is the Ukraine now."

Suddenly it hit me. "You're a Cossack!"

He blushed again, his dark eyes sparkling with amusement. "Does this please you?"

"A little," I had to admit. Anthropology had been my focus in the short term of college I had attended. My focus had been on military-based tribes. I'd written an entire paper on the people who had pretty much established the culture of modern day Russia, otherwise known as the Cossacks, and how their mobile culture eventually had a hand in the creation of the Romani people. I looked at him with his sparkling eyes and curling hair, and I couldn't figure out how I hadn't known what he was before.

"I'm glad."

He was flirting. Call me slow, but I hadn't realized it before. He was good at it, or at least good at the subtly of it. His bicep flexed beneath my grip as he opened up a heavy door of dark wood, and I stepped into what I can only call Heaven. Now I knew how Belle must have felt. There were two stories of wall-to-wall books. The covers ranged from antique leather to the modern paperback and everything in between. Comfortable plush chairs had been scattered here and there, including a big lounging couch in front of a fireplace that had already been lit.

"Holy crap," I said.

"Do you have a favorite author? A favorite book?" he asked.

I shook my head. "What's that line from *Ever After*? 'I could no sooner choose a favorite star in the sky?' Something like that."

"What is *Ever After*?"

"A movie," I answered, "A really cute movie. A re-imagining of the Cinderella story with Drew Barrymore. I love it."

"Then, I would like to see it."

"We could do that for our date?" I suggested. I took one of the aisles of books at random, pausing every now and then to run my fingers over one of the spines. I didn't know half the languages that some of these books were in, but they were still pretty to look at.

He gave me an uncertain glance. "You wouldn't want something more...spectacular?"

I laughed and shook my head. "Like what? Horse-drawn carriage and princess gowns? I mean, those things are cool and I totally wouldn't turn them down, but dates aren't always about extravagance, you know? Sometimes, they are more about spending time with someone doing something you can both enjoy.

 A night in with a great romantic movie and some takeout? Just add in a kitten on my feet and that's pretty much my definition of the perfect night in." I pulled one of the books off a shelf and opened to the first page, letting my eyes roam over some of the words without actually reading them.

He smirked. "A kitten?"

I shrugged. "I'm a witch, right? Shouldn't I have a cat and a pointy hat and that really big cast iron pot thing?"

"Cauldron," he supplied.

"Yeah, that's the one." I put the book back on the shelf and continued down the aisle. "How about you pick a book for me?"

He raised his brow at me. "Really?"

"Dude, I could be here all night and never choose, and I am already starting to get fuzzy in the brain stem. You pick one that you think that I would like, and I'll read it. Then, on our date, we can talk about it."

He grinned, and I felt my stomach melt all the way to my toes. He really was cute as hell, even with the pointy teeth. Maybe, I admitted silently, because of them. "What kind of books do you enjoy?"

"Well, normally, I like romantic books, but I think I've got plenty of that in my life right now. A good mystery or something would be nice. Something about a woman finding herself or whatever."

"Or whatever," he repeated, but the smile grew. "I think that I can find something to your tastes. Why don't you go sit on the couch?" He motioned to the long couch. "You are stumbling a little when you walk."

"Tired," I explained, feeling a little embarrassed. I wandered away from the shelves and plopped down on the lounging couch, toeing my feet out of my shoes and letting them clatter to the ground.

Okay, I had to admit that I liked him. Dmitri was really cute and sweet, and he liked books. What more could a girl like me ask for? Oh, well a killer body would be nice...and, uh, check?

He came back to me, a book in his hand.

"What's that?" I asked.

"This is Agatha Christie."

"I've never read her," I admitted. My head was heavy; I didn't want to lift it off the cushion. "I think I'm too tired to read her right this second. I'm sorry."

"Shh," he said, "I will read it to you."

Any other time, it would have been a weird thing to say, but right now? Having a book read to me by a Ukrainian vampire sounded like just the thing. "Okay."

I was asleep before he was done with the first page, but his voice was like music.

CHAPTER SEVEN

On the plus side, I woke up the next morning in my own clothes and in the same place that I had fallen asleep. Someone had even pulled a blanket over my legs so that I stayed warm after the fireplace had gone cold. On the bad side, I hadn't moved all night, so my neck felt like someone was shoving a chisel into it. I sat up and tilted my head from one side to the other in the hopes of alleviating some of the pain.

A book clattered to the floor, and I recognized it as the one that Dmitri had been reading to me when I had zonked out next to him. A piece of paper fluttered to the ground. I picked it up and my cheeks went instantly pink.

It was a quick sketch of me done with a bit of charcoal. Expert fingers had captured my unconscious face as if I were some kind of sleeping beauty.

There was a quote down at the bottom of it. "I had seen the princess and let her lie there unawakened, because the happily ever after was damnably much work."

I laughed and I wasn't even sure why, but it made me deliriously happy. A happy tingling started in my stomach, and warmed me all the way down to my toes. *Oh no,* I thought, *I was totally crushing on Dmitri. Jeez. What the heck was wrong with me? One nice evening and already I was having squishy feelings about an immortal vampire.*

Wait, I realized, they were totally immortal. Every last one of them. What the heck was I supposed to do? Fall in love and then grow old and die, while they remained perpetually perfect? That popped a hole in my balloon, and this time, I didn't have a grumpy vampire to blame for ruining my happy feelings. Great.

There was a very polite knock at the door and I blinked. "Uhh...yes?"

The door opened, and there stood Peter with a silver tray in one hand, and what looked like a fancy notecard in the other.

"Good morning, Miss."

"Hey," I said, drawing my legs up, feeling a little self-conscious. "Sorry, I didn't mean to fall asleep here. It just got...late."

He smiled gently down at me. It was the kind of smile I had always imagined a good father ought to have. That sort of quirk of the lips that managed to say, without words, that everything was alright. "Do not fret. You are not the first of the house's denizens to find comfort in front of the library fire. I have fixed you breakfast, or rather lunch."

I winced. "Jeez, is it that late?"

"In fifteen minutes it will officially be after noon."

It wasn't the latest that I had slept. I had worked closing shifts at the restaurant, but it was pretty close. "Wow, I'm sorry."

He smiled again and placed the tray at the end of the couch. It was a cheese omelet , served with some kind of hash browns.

"I hope this is acceptable. I still am not well versed in your dietary requirements."

"Oh," I said, picking up the fancy fork, "I'm pretty easy. As long as it's not loaded with onions or nuts, I'll be happy. I don't like onions, unless it's French Onion Soup. God, I can never get enough of that. But I'm allergic to tree-nuts."

"Understood."

"But seriously, you don't have to wait on me. I'm not really...used to it."

He shook his head. "I am more than happy to, Miss. It's been many years since I had anyone but vampires to wait upon, and they don't much appreciate my cooking."

I frowned and took a bite of eggs so light and fluffy they were basically air, and perfectly melted cheese. This was something I could get accustomed to quickly. "I thought vampires could eat?"

"They can, but many choose not to. Master Wei still enjoys his teas, and Master Alan will eat any sweet I create, but I enjoy having someone actually depend upon my food. That is the way of Brownies, I'm afraid. It's our nature."

There was a name I was familiar with. "The Fae?"

His eyes glittered. "You know of my kind?"

"Disney and I were buddies growing up. I know a little bit about that kind of thing. I know that Brownies are good fairies, and that they like to make things?"

"It is as good a definition of my people as any other I have seen. We like to care for the people that we enjoy the company of. We grow easily attached."

"Are you attached to the guys?" I asked.

He bowed his head. "They have their own charms. Speaking of the Masters..." he passed the notecard to me.

The handwriting on it was fancy, with loops and swishes that would have been right at home in the font section of an invitation maker. Turned out that I was right on the mark, because it was definitely an invitation to dinner that night with Alan.

"Lovely Lorena,

Would you do me the great honor of attending dinner with me tonight? I promise that it will be a night beyond compare, worthy of your dreams.
Yours, Alan"

Wow, I thought, *he certainly was full of himself.* I wasn't a fan of empty arrogance. If someone could live up to their boasting, I could appreciate it, but most guys who promised the world could only be counted on to give a square mile of swamp.

I raised my brow. "Is he for real?" I muttered, taking another bite.

"Master Alan is most serious in his desire to impress."

"I bet." I wasn't sure that anything could match Dmitri's quiet flirtation, but whatever. I had made a promise to let them both try, and I was going to do my best to live up to that. In the meantime, I was going to practice magic. An idea struck me. "Hey, Peter? Is there a place that I could work on my witchy-ness? Somewhere that I won't be a bother and that I won't be bothered by accident?"

He thought about it for a moment. "I think I have just the place."

I hurried up the rest of my breakfast and stood up. "Will you show me?"

He bowed his bald head again. "Absolutely."

He let me gather up my shoes and the book and then lead me up some stairs and to a room on the furthest side of the house. The moment I saw it, I was in love. Unlike the rest of the house, there were big windows, big arching ones that were taller than I was. They flooded the entire room with warm natural light that brought out the warm tones in the wooden floor. The room was surprisingly empty, with only a chandelier in the very center of the ceiling.

"It's perfect. What was it?"

"It was a music room at one point in time, back when Master Zane was still in residence."

"Who?" I asked.

"The fourth brother of the boys."

"There's another one?" I asked. "Why hadn't I been told before?"

"He has been missing for quite some time. It is assumed that were he able to come back, he would have."

It was the nicest way that I had ever heard "we think he's dead." It made me feel a little sorry for the group. It had to be hard enough living forever, but losing someone you thought was always going to be there had to be even worse.

"That sucks."

"Succinctly put, Miss. Will this do?"

"It's perfect."

He left me alone to work on my magic. I went back down to my bedroom to shower and change, grab the books that Jenny had picked out for me, and my phone. I had a few texts from her, and one from my father. I responded to hers, but didn't bother with Dad's. What was there to say? I forgive you for lying to me my entire life? Nope. Not gonna happen.

I plopped myself down on the floor, opened my grandmother's grimoire, and started to read.

"A witch," it said, "can see into the world of magic. The name for this realm varies depending on the place and language of the practitioner, but I have always called it The Weave. The first task for

76

any witch is to learn how to see it and become always aware of its presence."

"Yeah," I snorted, "that sounds easy enough."

I folded my legs beneath me and scooted across the floor until I could rest my back against the wall. The book described relaxing one's eyes until they were open, but asleep. This might have sounded strange to other people, but I had pretty much mastered that ability during math classes. I despised math.

"Okay, let's do this."

I plopped my hands down on my knees and started to breathe deeply, pushing it all the way to the very bottom of my lungs, and then blowing it out as slowly as I was able. I did it again and again until I wasn't thinking about it anymore. I rested my head back on the wall and looked out the massive windows to what lay beyond.

They were gardens, I realized, massive ones. There was a small brick courtyard in the very center with a large fountain at its most northern point. The fountain fed into what looked to be a pond. Around all of that was a series of perfect circles with what must have been thirty different kinds of plants all snuggled up with one another. A breeze teased the leaves, making them dance and sway in the afternoon sunlight. I let my entire body rest, relaxing one part of me after another until I wasn't aware of anything but my mind.

I thought it was some trick of the light at first, a line of color across my vision. It was the softest shade of blue I had ever seen, almost silvery. It ran through the glass like a spider's web, perfect, and yet pliant. I wanted to reach out for it. The moment that I thought it, it bent towards me, harkening to my unspoken command.

Suddenly, I could see a hundred other beams of light; not all of them were silvery. The ones that slipped through the wood were a lush brown, the ones in the leaves of the plants were verdant and thick. I knew that a squirrel was curling its gray body around one of the trees, even though I couldn't see him with my eyes. I could see the lines of deep brown magic coursing through him.

I looked down at myself and nearly gasped. My whole body was a series of spirals of what I assumed was The Weave. The cords of magic extended throughout my entire person, all in shades of copper and gold. Where the silver thread that extended from the window touched me, the spirals unfurled, jumping to touch the line of magic, sort of like those tesla ball things you saw in tech-shops. They combined, one line wrapping over the other until I couldn't tell where one started and one ended. Energy that I could almost taste built in that connection, and I was sure I could do something with it. What? I didn't know, but something.

I gave it a tug, using my hands to pull at something only I could see. At first nothing happened, just a hum along the skin, and then it shattered. Not the connection; I still held that in my hands, but the window exploded inwards as if someone had thrown a big rock through it. The thought was so real in my head that I immediately looked around for a slab of stone.

All I saw was glass.

It took me a full minute to realize that it had been me. I had broken the glass from all the way across the room.

A second later, Peter knocked on the door. I don't know how I knew it was Peter. It wasn't just that it was daytime, and I was pretty sure that he was the only one awake in the house besides myself, but I could...feel him. His magic was as rich as earth. I could almost smell herbs and spring dirt on the air as I turned towards the door.

"Yeah?" I called.

"Are you alright, Miss?" he pushed open the door, real concern coloring his face.

"Uhhh...I'm okay. The window? Not so much."

He glanced at the pile of glass that decorated the wooden floor like shattered diamonds. An outside breeze pumped through the room, carrying with it the scent of autumn. I was surprised that the sunlight, which had been high in the sky when I had started this, was touching the horizon. How long had I been sitting there?

"I see."

"I'm sorry," I said suddenly, and the Weave faded from my vision. Peter looked like Peter, and there were no threads of magic everywhere. "Holy crap, I didn't mean to do that."

He chuckled. "There is no use crying over spilt magic, Miss. I can clean this up."

I blinked in surprise. "You can?"

"I am a Brownie. Tending the home is my gift."

He held his hands out and the glass rose off of the floor. Another wave of his fingers and the shards all flew back into place, settling into the framework of the window. The pieces melted together as if they had never been broken in the first place.

"Holy crap," I repeated.

"You will be able to do similar things...unless your magic is inherently destructive."

I shrugged. I didn't know what my magic was other than unwieldy. "I...think that's enough for today."

"As you wish, Miss."

CHAPTER EIGHT

When I got back to my room, there was a dress waiting for me. It was hanging up on the edge of the dressing screen. It was red and black and clingy. I touched the fabric, and I knew that it was probably worth more than any paycheck I had ever received. Then, I saw the box and knew that I was in for it.

It was one of those long wide boxes that rich women kept their jewelry in. Most of my jewelry had come from thrift stores. With uncertain fingers, I popped open the box and nearly dropped it. Diamonds winked up at me from some kind of black metal, making them look like stars against a curling night sky. There were earrings and a bracelet to match.

"What the heck are we doing?" I wanted to know.

I had never been on a fancy date before. The closest that I had ever gotten was my junior prom, and that had pretty much been a bust. Mostly because my date had spent the entire time trying to get his hands on *my* bust, and when that hadn't worked out, he'd turned his attention to a friend's. Not exactly good memories.

I was a little nervous. Okay, scratch that. I was a lot nervous. I didn't know what to do with myself in that kind of outfit. What the heck was I going to do with my hair? I had the bare minimum of make-up, and this was definitely the kind of dress that you gussied up for.

In an act of hope and desperation, I sent a single word text to Jenny. "Help."

~~

"There are even shoes!" she exclaimed twenty minutes later, "Cute shoes."

I had to agree. The heels were more sensible than I would have thought after seeing the necklace. Simple black ones with a strip of glitter across the ankle and the toes. I wondered if those diamonds were real, too. They certainly glittered like they were.

"Okay, so lemme get this right." She flopped over on my bed, stretching out like a big warm brown cat. She held one of the shoes in one hand, and the box of jewelry in the other. "You done agreed to let all the boys take you out?"

"Well, the invitation is open, but Wei isn't having it."

She stuck her tongue out and rolled her eyes. "He stupid, anyway."

I chuckled and shook my head. "I don't think he's stupid. I think he just doesn't...like the idea of being beholden to prophecy."

She shrugged. "Well, ya got that in common."

I guessed we did. I hadn't thought of it that way. I smirked and shook my head. "It doesn't really help me with tonight."

"What can I do?"

"Can you do hair?"

She snorted and swished her head back and forth so that her braids swayed, the bits of crystal glittering. "What'choo think?"

"I beg your help."

"Take a seat." She rolled off the bed and motioned to the vanity. "You gonna tell me 'bout the big magic you casted?"

"Can you tell?" I asked, slipping into the seat.

"You smell like magic."

"I broke a window. I don't know if that counts as big magic. It was kind of an accident."

I told her the entire story, describing everything I could in detail while she worked a completely different kind of magic on my short mop of hair. For the first time since I had chopped it all off, I wished I had kept my long ash brown curls. Oh, well.

"You got any products?" she asked.

I opened a drawer in the vanity, showing her the paltry selection of styling products I had. It consisted of some soft hold hairspray and goop that I would use before shifts at work to hold my hair under my hat while I sweated like a pig.

She smirked. "I can work with this."

"You are a goddess."

She grinned. "True. But yeah, you worked some damn big magic. It's not as easy as people think to break things with magic. The Weave likes ta be where it's supposed to be. Pulling at it like you did? Big stuff."

I hadn't known that. Maybe because I didn't know it was easy for me, or maybe I had a knack. I wasn't sure which. Heck, I was pretty much not sure of anything. Great place to be.

"Neat. I can make really big messes. Magical."

She snorted and tugged her fingers through my hair, leaving a thin trail of product in their wake. She held her fingers there, so that when she released it, the hair fell in cute waves around my face. The effect was pretty elegant, if simple.

"Yesterday, you couldn't even see The Weave. Today, you can cause it to go against its own nature. Yeah, that's a big deal."

Well, when she put it like that, I felt pretty sheepish.

"Is this the first date?" she wanted to know as she moved to the other side of my hair.

"Kinda? I dunno, Dmitri and I had a... moment."

Her eyes caught mine in the mirror. "Didn't I tell ya he was somethin' else?"

I grinned my agreement and then told her about the whole night.

She sighed dramatically. "If only he was a she."

I reached up and patted her hand. "I'm sorry, sweetie."

She shrugged. "I'll find someone."

I really hoped she did. I had only known her for a couple of days, but already I was firmly in her corner of support. She deserved everything and then some.

"Damn right you will. Even if I have to gather up every lesbian on the mountain and bring her to your front door."

She stuck her tongue between her teeth and chuckled. "Don't be stupid. Okay...let's do your make-up."

Half an hour later, I looked like a CoverGirl version of myself. I did a little turn in front of the full-length mirror and took a deep breath. "Holy crap."

"He's gonna want to sink his fangs into you."

"Do they do that?" I asked, "Like, I know that the stories all say that, and they got the pointy teeth and...well...yesterday morning there was this moment but...crap, they totally do that, don't they?"

She nodded at me. "They totally do. I hear it feels good."

I remembered how much my body had ached for Alan to taste me yesterday, and Dmitri's response to the near bite.

"Yeah, that's what I hear." I swallowed.

The door opened, and Jenny and I both jumped. I expected to see Alan standing there, or maybe Dmitri, though I couldn't imagine him being rude enough to just open my bedroom door. It was neither. Instead, Wei stood there, his big shoulders filling the doorway. His eyes swept over me, from head to toe. He didn't say anything, just looked.

"Problem?" I asked.

"Alan says he's ready."

I raised my brow, surprised that he was bringing that bit of information to me. I couldn't really imagine Wei being anyone's messenger boy.

"I'll be down in a moment."

"You can tell him that yourself."

"So what, you can bring his message to me, but can't be bothered to respond?"

He lifted his chin arrogantly. "It was either I do it or Dmitri. I am not cruel enough to send Dmitri to see you walk into the arms of another man dressed as you are."

I blinked. When he put it like that, I felt kind of bad.

"I'll go," Jenny said, putting a hand of support on my shoulder, "You look great."

"Thanks," I answered and watched her go. Wei still stood there.

"What?" I asked again, feeling irritated. God, he got under my skin. "What is it?"

He took a deep breath. I wondered why. I was pretty sure that the vampires didn't need to breathe. "Do not draw this out. If you are going to pick, do it quickly."

I didn't have any plans of dangling the guys, that wasn't really my way. There were some people out there who liked having multiple partners. That was cool, so long as they weren't lying about it. Me? I just wanted one guy. Just one person that I could depend on. A guy who was as much my friend as he was my lover. I didn't think that was asking too much.

"I promised them both the chance. I intend to keep that promise."

"Why?" he wanted to know.

I blinked in surprise. "Because...you are supposed to keep promises?" I answered. *What kind of weird question was that?*

"You do not honor your parents, but you honor a promise?"

I rolled my eyes at him. "Dude, I explained this to you last night. My parents have done nothing in my life that has made me want to honor them."

"Your father cared for you, provided for your life."

"Yeah, because the law demands it of him. Besides, that's the bare minimum as far as I'm concerned, and no one gets a pat on the back for doing the absolute least shitty thing that they can do. He never bothered to try to help me when I struggled, or gave the least bit of a damn about my hopes and my dreams. He just expected me to listen to him and never to talk back. That's a dictator, not a parent. Okay?"

He frowned at me or maybe it was at himself. It wasn't his usual grumpy-face but something more introspective. "So, people who learn who you are? Who support you..."

"Those people? I will go to the wall for. Anyone who I can count on knows that they can count on me, too. Like Jenny. If that girl needed a kidney, I'd give it without even asking why."

"You do not know her."

I shrugged. "It doesn't matter. With some people, you just know."

I stood up, and he watched me. I wasn't blind, and even though he usually looked either grumpy or stoic, I could see the heat entered his eyes as I walked towards him.

"My respect has to be earned," I explained, "but the moment that it is? It's pretty damn hard to lose."

"I do not agree with that view...but I can respect it."

Then, he bowed. Really bowed. Like his hands stayed at his sides and he put his body in a deep graceful dip that was a sweep of motion that struck me breathless.

Prickly boy' I thought to myself, *but there was something there.* I just didn't really know what that something was.

"Thank you."

"Your date awaits."

He moved out of my way, letting me pass by. I paused in the hallway and looked over my shoulder at him. "Hey, I don't really want to be involved in this prophecy either. But I am making the best of it. I won't ask you to take part. That's not cool, but I'll let you know that the invitation is still open if you want to get to know me."

He watched me with the cool unblinking stare of a hawk. I could feel the gaze as I walked away.

CHAPTER NINE

If I looked good, Alan looked like a dream. I had to hand it to the guy, he really knew how to dress, or maybe he just knew how to present himself. When I came downstairs, he was lounging in an elegant antique wingback chair that I figured he chose to be the perfect background to his all too pretty self.

"Wow," I said.

He wore the same colors as I did; black, red, and silver, but the style was completely his own. The jacket, cut in that long aristocratic style, was a deep black velvet with silver stitching that fit him in just the right way to show off the elegant slenderness of his body. The ruffled red shirt he wore should have looked flamboyant, but he pulled it off, though maybe the black vest he wore helped with that.

The pants, equally black, were fitted slacks and skimmed the tops of his boots so perfectly that I knew they were tailored. Diamonds shimmered at his cuffs, the pin of his cravat, and a single one at one ear.

He smiled at me, bowing so that the tips of his blond hair swept against the ground. He hadn't pulled it back as far as I could tell, but it looked fancy enough just sitting there. He extended his hand to me like this was some romantic movie moment. Maybe it was.

"And you, Lorena Quinn, you look like a dream."

I placed my hand in his offered one. I was surprised to feel nothing but skin. With everything else he wore, I expected there to be the hat and gloves and everything, but all I felt was the satin caress of his fingers against mine as he lifted my knuckles to his lips. I couldn't help myself; I shivered. A shock of interest went from where his lips touched to all the places that liked to feel good.

I had to clear my throat before I could respond, because I'm super smooth that way. "I'd say thank you, but you picked everything out for me."

"I hope that I didn't overstep myself."

I shrugged. Maybe he had a little bit, but not so much that I was really bothered. He hadn't pinned a creepy note to the hanger that said "wear this or else" or something weird like that. *Red flag much?* "Well, if the dress had been ugly, I wouldn't have worn it."

His chuckle was so warm that it brought a tingle to my skin. It was like the elegant rumble of an instrument warming up.

His fingers were cool and strong against mine as he gave my hand the gentlest of squeezes. "You are a bewitching woman, Lorena."

"Well, to be fair, I am a witch."

He laughed. His laugh was even better. The chuckle was controlled, soft and pretty. The laugh was bright and unfettered. His lips spread enough that I could see the tips of his fangs. The points should have ruined his aesthetic...they didn't.

"What is it about a woman of wit?" He shook his head and kissed my knuckles again. I was expecting the zing this time, but it was no less potent. "Shall we?"

"Where are we going?" I asked, realizing that I had absolutely no clue what to expect from the night.

"How do you feel about French cuisine?"

"Honestly? I don't know much about it. Are there snails involved?" I liked to consider myself adventurous, but I drew the line at snails.

He took my hand and pressed it to the crook of his arm. It lacked the definition of Dmitri's bulk, but had its own slender elegance that I appreciated.

Ugh, I thought to myself, *I really needed to stop comparing them to one another.* That felt...unfair somehow. I didn't really want to turn this into some kind of pro-con competition, but what else was I supposed to do? Marry them all? Props to the polyandrous crowd, but I just didn't have that in me.

"From time to time," he admitted, "but the real power of French dining is the pleasure of wine."

I gave him a look. "Uh, rules might have changed since the last time you took a girl out for an evening of revelry or whatever, but I'm nineteen, I can't drink."

He patted the tops of my fingers. "While that is true in America, you are old enough to drink in France."

The meaning behind his words hit me like a ton of bricks. "Woah, wait a minute. What? Are we going to France?" My mouth didn't quite hang open, but it was pretty close.

"I promised you the time of your dreams, *ma cher.* I boast, but never exaggerate."

He led me outside, and for some reason, I was surprised to see a red and yellow helicopter there. I don't know what I expected to get to France on. At this point, a carriage drawn by flying horses would not be outside the realm of possibility. Was he serious? Was this actually happening? Also, could a helicopter make it across an ocean? Because I didn't think that was possible.

"Are we going to France in that?"

"*Non,* we are taking this to the airport, and from there, we are taking my private jet."

"Of course, we are," I said as he helped me into the co-pilot's seat, "that's normal."

He chuckled again, and I decided that I liked amusing him. It saved him from looking too perfect, even though he managed to do it without showing off any fang, unlike the laugh. Was that on purpose? Was he trying to look human? I wished I was comfortable enough to ask him.

"It is for me."

Now, that I believed. He had probably been born rich in the era when having wealth made you a god among peasants or whatever. French history was not my area of expertise, but they had that pretty intense revolution because the aristocracy got just a little too aristocratic.

"How are you guys so rich? As far as I can tell, none of you work."

"That is not entirely accurate," he said as he tapped the door shut and then went around to his side. He hefted himself into the pilot's seat with far more grace than I would have been able to do and handed me a helmet. I was suddenly thankful to my years of fast food that taught me how to handle ugly hats and cute hair. His next comment came through the headset. "Dmitri sells his paintings. They bring in a relatively decent amount of money. I own several of my own businesses."

"What about Wei?" I couldn't imagine grumpy Wei doing anything but bossing people around.

"He's a carpenter when the mood strikes him."

I frowned. "Do they make a lot of money?"

Alan shrugged and began messing with buttons until the blades above us started to spin. A heavy breeze puffed through the cockpit. "His last commission went for the better part of a million dollars."

"Jeez," I whispered, "I've never made more than fourteen thousand in a year."

He chuckled. "That's a very American view of you."

"What?"

"For a land of the free, it has always struck me how expensive it is to live in your country. And never have I been more aware of what the phrase 'earn a living' is than when I have been within your borders."

That thought kept me distracted as the helicopter lifted up and the world surged away from us. We were twenty minutes up when he asked me if I wanted to drive.

"Oh no, it took me three years to get my license. I'd rather we didn't die in a ball of helicopter fire."

He laughed at me again. I'm glad I amused him so much. I remember reading somewhere that if you liked someone, you laughed at their jokes more. Some weird little quick of socialization. Maybe he was just crushing on me. Yeah, right.

I was pretty sure me going to France without a passport was illegal, but I was also pretty sure that Alan had pulled some very interesting strings. He handled the helicopter the same way he seemed to handle everything else, with a seamless sort of elegance that I could only dream of having. When we went from the landing pad at the airport to the runway, he strutted around as if he owned everything that he could see.

The jet he led me to was, for lack of a better description, state-of-the-art. It was sleek and white and looked more like a space age bullet than any plane that I had ever seen.

"What is it?" I asked.

"A plane of my own design."

"You design planes?" I asked, wondering if my mouth was actually hanging open or if I just felt slack-jawed. Alan surprised me on a lot of levels.

"It is one of my businesses, yes. I call this beauty the Roc, based on the epic bird of Native American legend. It flies at around two thousand miles per hour. It is not quite as fast as the Blackbird, the military jet, not the creature. Right now, it is too expensive to build and maintain for the average airline, but my people are looking to convert it."

"Of course, they are," I said as he led me up the short series of steps towards the jet.

"Hello, Sir," a snappily dressed man greeted us, "we have already begun preparations and will be taking off as planned. Would you like any inflight beverages?"

Alan looked at me, and I shook my head. All the flying left me feeling a little uncertain in the stomach region.

"No, thank you, James. We will just take our seats."

"As you wish, sir."

Alan led me to a plush white seat that made me feel like I was sitting on a marshmallow. I pulled the seatbelt on and, partway through, realized the chair swiveled. A few weeks ago, I had been struggling to pay my phone bill, and now, I was sitting in a swivel chair on a dream.

"I'm dreaming," I blurted out, "That little magic trick knocked me out, and I am hallucinating this entire thing. I'm almost sure of it."

Alan smirked at me, taking the seat to my right. "What makes you say that, Lorena?"

"This is the kind of thing that only happens in my dreams or very particular daydreams. Some hot immortal dude with a zillion dollars swoops in and treats me like some princess. I mean, that doesn't happen."

He lounged comfortably in his seat, curling his fingers beneath his chin and eyeing me in a way that I could only describe as careful. He reminded me of a cat, cautious and sleek. "It's happening now."

"Yeah." I blew out a deep breath. "Yeah, I guess it is."

"Is something wrong?" His voice was completely empty of emotion. His lips formed a line that would have been a smile were it not for the polite emptiness of the rest of him.

"I'm gonna screw this up," I blurted before I could stop myself, "I've been on dates before, don't get me wrong, but this is...dude, this is something else."

"Did you just call me...dude?"

"See!" I cried out, tossing my hands into the air, "I am not a cool and proper princess who knows how to handle herself on fancy dates. Heck, my date to prom took me to Taco Bell. I don't know what to call you or what to talk about or...I don't even know where we are going. The only place in France I know about is Paris."

His lips stayed fixed in that empty smile, and I wasn't sure if that was a good sign or not. He remained quiet for a full minute, looking at me as if waiting for me to do something. His eyes were blue. I hadn't noticed before. The rest of him was so damn pretty that sometimes it was hard to notice the eyes. They were the softest shade of blue with tiny flecks of gray and silver in them. They were different from that time he had almost ensnared me with his vampire magic.

"I intimidate you," he said after a moment.

I blew out another breath. "A little."

"We aren't going to Paris," he told me, "Is that disappointing?"

"No, not at all," I promised. I meant it. The idea of going to that really big city with all of those tourists just didn't interest me at all. I wouldn't call myself an introvert or anything, but large groups weren't my thing. Large groups while I wore a fancy dress and was out on a first date with the hottest dude ever, trying desperately not to spill anything on myself, was a whole category of "please don't."

"Where are we going?" I asked him.

"A little town just outside of Marseille called Alluch."

I struggled with the names. I really should have taken French in high school. "Okay, why there?"

He hesitated for second and then said, "It is where I was born."

Shock rendered me speechless. Why was he taking me there? It seemed very...intimate. I closed my mouth and then opened it several times until I felt like a fish.

He laughed. It was a loud and rolling sound, so unfettered that I saw the fullness of his fangs. He laughed for a full minute before he finally began to ease. "Do not look so stricken, *ma Cher,* I will not be introducing you to my mother and father. I assure you that they have been gone for quite some time."

Well, duh. I didn't say it, but I was sure I thought it loud enough that he could see it on my face. His grin remained large enough that his fangs were sharp points at the corners of his lips.

"Were they the lords of the province?" I asked, trying to do anything but sit there and stare at him dumbly.

He shook his head and straightened his jacket in a gesture I might have called nervous with anyone else. I couldn't imagine Alan feeling anything as mundane as nervous. "*Non.* My father was a fisherman, and my mother was a laundress."

I blinked. Apparently, my moments of being shocked were just beginning tonight. We were both quiet as the plane began the final take-off procedures. We didn't speak again until the jet, whose engines sounded like a billion tigers roaring, settled above the clouds. Alan was back to looking like a mildly bored cat.

"I didn't..." I fumbled, "Dude...I do not know how to talk to you."

He reached across the space between us. His pale marble-like fingers slid across my warm ones. He turned my hand over until my palm was upright, and pressed his palm flatly to mine. "You talk well enough with Dmitri."

I flushed deeply. "He's easy to talk to."

Alan nodded, his gaze not meeting mine. "He is. And beautiful, too. The sweet-faced artist with the intoxication of a creative temper. It is a heady comingling of personality. He is, I think, everyone's favorite. Including my own."

I tilted my head. There was something about the way that Alan spoke about Dmitri. It wasn't the typical kind of bro talk I was used to one guy using for his best buddy. It was...gentler than that. A thought hit me, but I couldn't bring myself to ask, at least not yet.

Instead I said, "We have a lot in common."

His fingers slid back and forth across my palm, tracing the natural lines there. "Ah yes, books have long bridged the gaps between people. I have always thought that bibliophiles shared their own language, a secret language of a people who partook of the same daydreams, who lived the lives of the same characters."

It was poetically accurate. "It does help. Do you read?"

He shook his head, his lips tilted in sadness. "When I was alive, really alive, books were a thing that only the wealthy might have. And my first few years as one of the creatures of the night were...difficult."

"Why?" I asked.

His fingers laced with mine. They were growing warmer, or maybe I was just growing used to their cool temperature. "The Change is very painful and...jarring...for some of us more than others."

"I'm sorry."

He shook his head, and started to pull his hand away, but I put my other one on top of it. He went very, very still. It wasn't the kind of stillness that a human being had, where they breathed or blinked or other micro-movements that we didn't really pay attention to. It was the kind of still that a doll could have or a dead body. I was reminded, quite suddenly, that he wasn't human. I was also reminded that he had been around, if not alive, for more years than I would ever see.

"Will you tell me what it's like? Becoming a vampire?"

He gave me a grin that lacked any amusement. I had never seen so many kinds of smiles on a single face. "Are you thinking about becoming one of the undead?"

I shrugged. It was close enough to the truth that I shifted in my seat. "I dunno. I mean, according to the Prophecy, I'm supposed to have the child of one of you three. And I'm sorry, but I'm just not going to have a kid with a guy I don't totally love. So...like...here I am with all these mixed feelings about being some girl of prophecy, but I know for sure that if I fall in love with one of you that means you guys are going to live forever while I grow old and die.

 And like, what about this prophecy kid? What if they don't wanna bring magic back into the world? What if they are so magical that they grow super quick? Or what if they don't grow at all? Like...what am I supposed to do?"

He curled his fingers around my hand. "You ramble when you are nervous."

"You should see me try to talk in front of a group."

"Is it that bad?"

"Hindenburg bad."

His grip tightened ever so slightly. I think he was trying to be comforting. "In order to be turned, a single vampire must drain a living person to the point of death three times. And then, when the third moment comes, and the heart beat is so slow that it is nearly nothing at all, the near-dead must drink over the course of three nights from the vein of Vlad himself."

I blinked. "So, you guys couldn't make me a vampire?"

He shook his head. "Not that I am aware of. Only Vlad and his brides have that ability."

I frowned. "Wait...how many vampires are there in the world?"

He thought about that. "There is Vlad himself and his three brides; Anja, Genevieve, and Yasmina. Each of the brides has a daughter. I believe their names are Aelwynn, Rehema, and Kateri. There is myself, Wei, and Dmitri. There are some mixed feelings about Zane and whether or not he lives."

He stopped. I waited for him to go on, but he didn't. "Wait, there are only eleven vampires in the whole world?"

"You have been told that magic wanes, have you not?"

I had, but I didn't understand what that had to do with such a low vampire population. "I thought vampires fed on blood, not magic."

"We survive on blood, the way you survive on food. But the lines of magic are more like...air. Right now, the air is very thin, thin enough that it cannot support others."

"What about other creatures? Werewolves and such?"

"There is only one clan of shape-shifters. Some of them are wolves. But there are also bears, swans, tigers, and panthers. I think they number in the fifties. They share a trailer park near the Canadian border, I think, though they also have a place in South Africa."

I was fascinated. "And witches?"

He smirked at me, and it was right around then that I realized that Alan used smiles the same way that other people used blank-face. It was his go-to expression when he wanted to hide what he was thinking; a mask of amused politeness. I wondered how I was going to learn more about him if he kept hiding behind the smirk, but I'd save that for later. It didn't feel like first date conversation.

"More of those, but not many. There are several families of witches, such as the Quinns and the Greens. But any person may become a witch should they learn how to tap into the Weave."

"Are all witches female?" I realized I hadn't seen a boy-witch, or even heard of one.

"Witch is a term without gender, though there was a time in which any wise woman might be labeled a witch, which is where we get the prejudice, I believe."

I opened my mouth to ask another question, and then snapped it shut. "I'm sorry."

He raised a single brow up his forehead that was the most honest expression I had seen him make so far tonight. Well, that and the laughing. The laughing had been excellent.

"What exactly are you apologizing for, *ma cher*?"

"Here we are, supposed to be on our way to the romantic date to end all romantic dates, and I'm over here pestering you with questions, showing off my complete lack of magical education or whatever."

"Firstly, let me just say that I believe that you and I might define 'pester' differently. I was under the assumption that we are having a conversation. As for the lack of magical education, as you so quaintly dubbed it, the fault cannot be pinned upon you. As far as I can tell, Lorena, you have a zest for understanding, one that I am...enthusiastic of."

He said enthusiastic the way other guys said horny. A new tingle surged up inside all the places I was too embarrassed to name. I looked down at our hands. I had almost forgotten that they were still linked together. "I asked 'why' a lot as a kid. I annoyed my father with it."

"I was much the same," he promised. "I had this unquenchable thirst for knowledge. I wanted to understand everything. If the sun was in the sky, I wanted to understand why. If the fish were biting, I wanted to know what made them do so."

"Me too!" I gushed, shifting around in my seat to face him better, "I remember this one time in kindergarten I found a book about dinosaurs, which was pretty much brand spanking new for me, so there I was, curled up in a corner, reading about giant flying lizard-birds and I just...I had so many questions. So, I walked right up to my teacher, who was in the middle of something else entirely, and I just started to ask one thing after another."

"Do you still read about dinosaurs?" he asked.

"I did until I started reading about dragons." I knew how I sounded, but I couldn't stop myself. "I remember the first time I heard about dragons. It was in this book. A girl finds this big egg in her backyard, and tries to hatch it, and it turns out to be a dragon and like...I must have read that book a zillion times. One of the apartments that we lived in had these great big trees out front. I wasn't supposed to climb on them, but one of the branches looked like a dragon neck. I couldn't help myself. I'd go up there and daydream about having a dragon friend of my own."

His hand gripped mine. "I am aware of your feelings on the subject, but I feel it is my place to tell you that there could be dragons again, should magic return to the world."

I swallowed so suddenly it very nearly hurt my throat. "Are. You. Serious?"

"I'd never lie about dragons."

I frowned at him. "Lemme guess, this is tied in with the magic-baby prophecy?"

He shrugged. "Dragons are great beings of magic. They cannot exist without a reawakening of the Weave."

He gripped my hand once more and then let it go. Maybe he sensed that I wanted to be alone with my thoughts, or maybe he felt that we had touched for far too long. Either way, I was happy for the space and the quiet to figure a few things out.

For as long as I had known about them, I had been fascinated by the idea of dragons. Giant flying lizards who could spit fire and carry me into the sky? Yes, please. Sign me up. And that daydream, born from the mind of the lonely girl I had been, could very well be mine if I would just, you know, fulfill the prophecy.

No pressure or anything.

~~

The restaurant was small, but classy. It sat on a hill overlooking the ocean and the apparently famous city of Marseille. I didn't speak a word of French, so I left it to Alan, who seemed more than happy to order everything for us. There were four different types of wine (apparently, the drinking age in France is 16) and crusty bread flavored with herbs. But the real centerpiece was the soup.

"Okay, what is this?" I asked after the third course had been removed from the table and replaced with a reddish-orange soup that had seafood bobbing around in it. I lifted my spoon and pushed a shrimp around in the broth. The scent coming off of it was the definition of mouthwatering as far as I was concerned.

"Bouillabaisse," he purred.

"Gesundheit." I brought a single spoonful of broth to my lips and took a sip. "Holy crap."

"Do you like it?"

Like it? It was the best thing I had ever tasted. What had I been missing all of my life? Oh, right. The money to afford fantastic food. Goodbye, chicken nuggets. "Oh, yes."

He nodded and swirled his own spoon through the broth. His lips were tilted into a somber line like he was remembering something that hurt. "This soup tastes like home, more than anything else for me. Since my father was a fisherman, we always had something to eat, so long as there were fish to be caught. My mother would make bouillabaisse frequently."

"Did you have any brothers or sisters?" I asked. It was clear that something was bugging him, and I didn't want to just ask him right out what was up, but I wanted to give him an opening to talk about it if he wanted to. That's me. Lorena Quinn, master of beating around the bush and creating awkward moments for all.

He shifted in his seat as if he was uncomfortable. I didn't think that was the case. The chairs were plush enough, and I don't think there was any actual blood flow to make his backside get tingly from being in the same position for that long.

Wait...if the dude didn't have any blood flow...uhhh...how was I supposed to...well...get pregnant? I might not have been a whiz in high school, but I passed sex ed. I decided to save that question for another time. Maybe Jenny would know.

"I had seven of them, and each of them was more tedious than the last." He picked up his glass, swirling the liquid around inside until it made a pale pink wave in the cup.

"Tell me about them." I took a sip of my own drink. I've gotta be honest. At first, I didn't like the flavor, but it kind of grew on me.

"Why?"

"First dates are all about getting to know one another," I explained. "At least, in the modern era."

He sighed softly. "Forgive me, *ma cher*. It has been some time since I have attempted to court a lady."

"Really?" I did my best not to sound surprised, really I did.

He gave me that humorless smile that I now knew meant he was hiding something. "Contrary to popular belief, Lorena, I do not have women in my room every night. In truth, I have not been on a date since my current ensemble was fashionable."

"I'm sorry."

"For what?"

I shrugged my shoulders, smoothing a nonexistent wrinkle in my skirt. "For making assumptions. I pretty much hate it when people make those about me. I mean, the moment that I tell people that I like comic books and video games, they automatically think that I'm awkward and socially impaired and don't integrate well with reality. The fact that they are right means absolutely nothing."

His laugh was a shock of sound. Yeah, I thought to myself, I'd do a lot of things to get Alan to laugh. Damn. I liked him, too.

"Now, how about you tell me about those siblings?"

He did, in as much detail as he could remember, and despite being undead for the past zillion years, he could remember a lot. Maybe vampires had good memories, or maybe it was just a quirk of his. I liked hearing about them. I didn't have any siblings of my own and had always been pretty much fascinated with the idea of them.

"Genevieve?" I asked as dessert was brought to our table, "Like the vampire?"

His lips took on a wistful curl. "My sister, both in life and as a vampire. She was seven years my senior and I adored her. Despite her lowly birth, or maybe because of it, she caught the attention of Vlad first. We were very close, and when he chose her to be one of his brides, she begged him to bring me along. I was eleven at the time, and he would not turn me for another ten years. But that, I think, is a story for another time."

"Are we going home?" I asked.

He gave me a long look. His emotions were hidden behind that mask again, and I knew that they were hiding something. Hope? Or something else?

"Do you want to go home?" he asked. His voice was careful, even neutral.

"How long do we have until sunrise?"

A look glimmered through his achingly pretty eyes. "A few hours."

"Then show me more."

We walked down the road on the edge of the beach, my arm linked through his. He showed me the buildings that had been in the village since he was alive, and the ones that had been added since then. As he talked, I began to understand the way he thought, the way he connected one memory to the next like some kind of stitch work. He was smart and suave and incredibly attractive. I noticed the way that other people noticed us. No one sneered, but I got the feeling that if

103

it had been anyone but Alan wearing antique finery, they might have.

Eventually, we made it down to the waterfront to the very spot where his home used to be. It was long gone, but a small house stood where it had been. It was quiet, and the moon was this massive disc of silver in the sky.

"I could live there," I said, eyeing the sea cottage. "I'd keep the windows open all day, just listening to the water and the wind."

"Were you to choose me, Lorena, I'd give it to you as a thank you gift."

I blinked at him. "What? Are you trying to bribe me?"

"Perhaps a little. I do not have Dmitri's creative charm, nor do I have Wei's power, but I would treat you like a princess, a goddess, or more if you would choose me."

For a moment, I couldn't breathe. I have never thought of myself as a greedy or superficial person, but it was really tempting to say yes to the super-hot dude who was offering my own house by the sea.

"Before I think too much of this...can I ask a question?" When he nodded, I continued. "If you weren't born noble, why all the fancy clothes?"

He eyed me. "Would you like to see me without them?"

I blushed, but bumped him with my hip. "I would have to be ten years dead not to want to see you naked, and even then, I am pretty sure my ghost would crawl back out of whatever afterlife she was cruising around in if you offered to do a nude shimmy on my grave."

"High praise." He ran his tongue across his teeth again. This time, I could see the elegant, slightly curved, points of his teeth.

"I call it like I see it." I shrugged. "It's true enough."

He paused at the end of the street. There were less lights here, and the ocean echoed around us. "All you have to do is ask."

I am smooth. So smooth. It's why I have a lot of dates. My mouth went dry. I swallowed hard enough that I was pretty sure I made that 'gulp' sound that you hear in cheesy Saturday morning cartoons. "Uhhh...what?" Yup, that's exactly how smooth I can be.

His hand slid up my very exposed arm, the tips of his fingers skimming over my bare shoulder, my neck, and then my chin. I had never been so aware of something as simple as a touch. Tingles shot from the places his fingers lingered to the parts of my body that started to ache.

"If you want to see me naked, Lorena, all you have to do is tell me what you want me to take off."

His thumb skimmed ever so lightly over my chin, the tip of his nail outlined the fullness of my lower lip. His fingers were electricity, guiding sensations with his touch. There was a part of me, dark and unexplored, that very much wanted to tell him to start taking off of his clothes. But I wasn't ready for that...and we were totally in public.

"Kiss me."

His lips parted ever so slightly. "Do you mean it?"

"It's been a fantastic date. I think it ought to end with a kiss."

"As you wish, *ma Cher.*"

His arms slid around me, pulling me gently closer. The ruffled edges of his shirt were not half as soft as they looked, but I liked the way they felt against my skin. I had never been so aware of my body as his palms skimmed along my cheeks, one staying there, the other dipping into the locks of my hair. For a moment we just stood there, his eyes looking into mine. Then, he dipped his head, and the moment our lips touched, I swear I stopped feeling my legs.

His lips were soft, softer than satin or silk or any fabric I could think of. They pressed easily at first and then harder until I was pretty sure fireworks were going off behind the eyes that I belatedly remembered to close. His tongue dipped against mine, and I felt my body go heavy with lust.

When he pulled back, I was surprised that I could breathe again. I was surprised that I wasn't a ball of mush puddling on the rocky beach, too, so there's that.

"Will that do, Lorena?"

I nodded slowly, not entirely trusting myself to speak.

"Come along then," he said, taking my hand in his, "We'll have to fly back soon."

It took me a moment to remember that I wasn't already flying, and I dimly wondered if that single kiss had ruined me forever.

CHAPTER TEN

It was her voice that woke me, even though I didn't realize it at first. Instead, I thought it was my phone. I 'd drank a little more wine on the plane trip home, and I was sleeping the deep and drool-filled sleep of the girl who was going to be experiencing her very first hangover in the morning. As I glanced at the clock on my phone, the light glared up at me with enough power that I thought I might be experiencing the hangover anyway. Since it was just shy of three thirty, I knew I had only been in bed for an hour. I also knew that I had no missed messages or phone calls or any alarm, and therefore, the phone could not be what woke me up.

"Uuugh," I said, rolling over. I think my head kept going. I brought one hand to my forehead to keep it from falling off the pillow.

"Lorena," the voice said, and it was right around then that I realized that I had heard it before.

I sat up in my big ol' princess bed, and through the bleary gaze of the not quite awake, I saw her. She looked pretty much the same as she had when she'd shown up at Ms. Marquesa's store, at least before she'd looked creepy. The gray robes large enough to mask the face beneath them, the elegant hand with the fingers of moonlight. Her presence didn't pack the same punch as it had that first night. I got the feeling she'd toned it all down, just for me. How nice. Yeah...

"What the heck are you doing here?" I asked. I didn't sound particularly polite. I really hate being woken up.

"I came to see you."

"Why?" It seemed like the right thing to ask, even though what I really wanted to do was pass back out and sleep through the headache I could already feel pressing behind my eyes.

"I'm allowed to see my daughter if I want to."

For a full minute, I didn't say anything. I was pretty sure I had fallen back asleep and was dreaming all of this. Better yet, maybe I had never woken up in the first place. This was all a dream. There was no way the woman in the gray robe was my mom. Right?

"You wanna run that by me again?" I asked. I pulled the blanket tighter around myself.

"I think you heard me the first time. Lorena, goodness, you have grown up so beautiful."

She pushed her hood back, and I felt my throat close.

My dad had kept almost nothing from his life before I was born. There were no pictures of my grandmother, no yearbooks with stupid "have a great summer" messages, or even prom snapshots. I remember this wild fantasy my overactive imagination had come up with, telling me that my dad was actually part of the witness protection program. When I asked him about it, he rolled his eyes and told me that I daydreamed too much. So much for that.

He hadn't kept much...but there was a single Polaroid of my mother. She wasn't much older than nineteen or twenty, her belly was swollen with itty-bitty me. She was laying out in a hammock, wearing a dress I would have called BoHo with a flower tucked into her blonde hair. I remember looking at it for hours, memorizing all of her features, wondering where I was in them. Because, despite the fact that she was my mom, I didn't look much like her.

The woman standing in my room, gray robes floating around her body like mist, totally did. A little older, with lines around her eyes and lips. Pretty, that much was true, but I had no desire to run to her arms and call her mommy.

"Okay, Vader, start talking."

Her eyes lit up with amusement. "You're funny, too."

"That's me." I drew my legs up, wrapping my arms around my knees beneath the blanket. "But I was asking about you."

She didn't move, but the image of her flickered. I should have known she wasn't really there. I mean, how many people could break into a house full of vampires...at night...while wearing floaty cosmic robes?

"What do you want to know?"

"Well, let's start with something easy. What the hell are you doing here?"

She gave me that kind of smile that I always pictured a mother might give her kid when they did something both idiotic and cute. "Sweetheart, I already told you. I wanted to see you. I haven't seen you in a very long time."

"Yeah?" I asked. Maybe it was the headache, maybe it was the surge of conflicting feelings, and maybe it was the fact that she was calling me some cheesy pet name; either way, I was feeling pretty grumpy. "Then where the heck have you been the past eighteen years?"

"Sweetheart..."

I held up a hand. "Stop. Listen. I don't mean to be a bitch here, but it's going to happen. If you are my mom, and I am reserving believing that one, by the way, then where have you been, and why are you showing up now?"

"I left, because your father and I disagreed about how we were going to raise you. I am here now, because you seem like you want to make your own choice, and I'm hoping you will hear my side of things."

It was the first thing so far that had made any sense. My dad was all about deciding things for me. "What's your side?"

"It's too complicated to talk about here."

"Gee, that's convenient." I rolled my eyes. What was she going to say next? That I had a long-lost sister? Then again, that probably wasn't totally outside the realm of possibility.

"Please, Lorena." She gave me another mom look, this one not nearly as amused as the other one. "I can't be here for long. The wards on this house are impressive."

"Are you a witch?"

She smiled at me, and the image of her flickered again. "Come to me, Lorena. Come see me."

The image flickered and then vanished completely. I sighed and flopped over. The headache was pounding now, and my head was filled to burst with heavy thoughts. *Was she my mom? Was she a witch? What did this have to do with me?* I was betting it had to do with this damn prophecy, too. Ugh. Just when I start to cozy up to the perks, something makes me rethink myself.

I threw the blankets back and pulled a robe over my shoulders. Sleep was apparently not going to happen right now. I thought about going downstairs and fixing myself a sandwich or something. Maybe read a few chapters of a book. I'd like to play a few levels of a video game, but there was no television where I could hook up my console.

Air, I thought to myself, *'some nice fresh air would feel good.'* It might even help with the headache. I opened the big stained glass door and stepped out onto the semi-circle balcony just outside. The moon was as full and bright here as it was in France. Seeing it hanging there, one big perfect globe, made me think of that little clan of shifters in Canada. Did they change with the moon? Or was that just a myth? I added that to the mental list of questions that I was steadily building.

A sound caught my attention. It was a door opening. A moment later, Wei stepped out and made his way to the very center of the courtyard. He was dressed in one of the martial arts uniforms that I was used to seeing him wear. This one was pure white, and it left his arms bare. The tunic, because what else could I call it, was long enough that the ends were slit at the thighs and hips to offer freedom of movement. He had a long straight blade with a short tassel on the hilt. His feet were bare.

I don't think he knew I was there. He started to...well...dance. Not dancing the way I would have done it. No one ever needed to see that. This was a martial dance, a smooth flowing of one move into another that made the long line of his pitch black hair move with him.

I couldn't help but watch. The fluid nature of his motions were hypnotic. and the headache began to ease. It helped that his arms and shoulders were...well...perfect. Everything about Wei, aside from his stoic arrogance and prickly nature, was.

The minute he knew I was there, his shoulders went tight. His motions faltered. He whirled around and looked up at me. Even from here, I could see the grim line of his lips.

"You should be sleeping."

I sighed. "You should be less of a jerk."

He frowned even harder at me, then he clapped his hands to his sides and gave me a short bow. "Forgive me. My words did not match my meaning. What I meant was, why aren't you asleep? Is there some problem?"

His words were clipped, and they didn't have any warmth in them. If he had been a little more open, I might have told him about my maybe-mom's visit. As it was, I offered him the best answer I could. "I have a headache." It was true enough, if not the entire truth.

He tilted his head to one side. "Do you get headaches often?"

I shook my head, and immediately regretted it. My palm was too warm against my forehead, and it made everything worse. "No, I think it was from the wine I had with dinner."

"Ah."

I had never known a single person to put so much distaste into a single syllable.

"Don't get snooty with me," I said, tugging the robe closer to me. I was in no mood for this and I said so. "I don't have the patience to deal with your prickly attitude."

He raised a brow at me. "Prickly?"

I leaned against the edge of the balcony. "You've been pretty prickly with me. I know you don't like me-"

"That is...not fair. I do not know you."

It was my turn to raise my brow at him. "That's weird, because you've been acting like I'm the scum of the Earth. I was racking my brain trying to figure out when I had run over your dog."

He made a sound I might have called a laugh if it had been coming from anyone else, but from Wei, it was more like enthusiastic throat clearing. "I do not hate you."

"Glad we cleared that up."

"I am... uncomfortable."

"Then come sit down," I said, completely missing the meaning of his words.

He frowned at me again. He was good at frowning. It suited him. But he bowed once more and then shifted his weight on his feet. I knew that he was going to leap an instant before it happened. I just didn't realize that a vampire could clear the two stories with a standing jump. He hovered in the air for a second, as if he could fly, and then landed on the balcony with the kind of grace I could only dream of having.

"I feel like I ought to applaud or something."

"That is not necessary."

I rolled my eyes, but halfway through, I realized that his lips weren't frowning quite so much as usual.

"Wait, did you just make a joke?"

He shrugged, and his arms did neat things that a romance novel might have called 'ripples'. He might not have Dmitri's overt muscles, but there was clear definition there that was hard not to stare at. Hard, but not impossible.

"I am capable of wit, I just choose not to use it."

That seemed completely foreign to me. I liked wit. I used it often, usually to keep from crying or yelling or any overt emotion. I was a completely functional human being, I swear. "Why?"

"Because people misunderstand things. I do not like being misunderstood."

I almost laughed. "That's weird, because I misunderstand you a lot."

"I have noticed." He sighed, and for the first time, he looked...tired. "Can I be blunt?"

"Do you know any other way to be?"

He shot me a look that would have looked annoyed were it not for the glimmer in his eyes. "I am not good with...this."

"With what?" I asked, leaning casually against the railing.

He let out the smallest sigh I had ever heard and said, "Women."

I did my best not to laugh. I swear I did, but I was operating on an hour's worth of sleep, wine was still humming in my system, and my long-lost mother (or a really good replica) had visited me via magic not ten minute before. *So, you know, I wasn't at my best.* "I'm sorry," I said when I stopped chuckling. "I just...that was pretty much the last thing I expected you to say."

"Why?" he demanded.

"Dude, I have seen you toss Dmitri and Alan around like they were foolish children. And even then, you barely ruffled your hair. You always seem so...controlled."

"You do not know me any better than I know you."

"It's not like you've made it easy to get to know you." I took an angry step in his direction.

"It is not as if you were trying to get to know me." He leaned over me, as if his scant inch or two of height would intimidate me. It might have worked if I wasn't feeling so terrible.

I threw my hands up. The pain behind my eyes had become a pulsing hammer. "I was trying to get to know everyone."

"Forgive me if I have no desire to be a number amongst your harem."

It wasn't fair, but it was a little true. "I don't have a harem. I'm not sleeping with anyone. And why do you care? Don't you want magic to come back into the world? Don't you-damnit," I snapped when the pain behind my eyes rendered me just a little blind. I placed my palms over my forehead and hoped the world would just stop spinning.

He watched me for a moment and then held his hand out. When I just stared at it dumbly, he said, "Give me your hand."

I did, only because I was too surprised not to. He turned it over so that the back of my hand fit into the curve of his palm. He ran his fingers over my skin, and I blinked. His touch was surprisingly gentle. He took the soft part of my hand between my thumb and forefinger and applied the smallest amount of pressure. The pain behind my eyes eased.

"Wow," I said after a moment.

He kept his hand there. I could almost feel a small tingle creeping up from the place where he touched and the pain in my head.

"Yes."

I blinked at him, wondering what he was responding to now.

"I want magic back," he continued. "I want to know what the world would be if the Weave pulsed and thrived the way it is described in the books of old."

He trailed off, looked away, and dropped his hand away from mine.

"But?" I prompted.

"But...I do not want to simply be the man who happened to be there at the time. If I take a woman, it will be because I love her, and she loves me, and the child we create will be...cared for. And, I hope you do not take this in the way that it was not meant, but I do not want to watch a woman I love wither away and die."

What did it say about Wei that he was saying the same things that I had been feeling?

I crossed my arms over my chest. "I didn't ask for this."

"But you have not shirked it either."

"What am I supposed to do?" I demanded suddenly. "I grew up reading stories about faeries and vampires and dragons and now I'm being told that I can see all of those things, that I can be a part in bringing back all the things that we think are fairytales. All I've got to do is have a baby with the right dude."

Tears I didn't know I had spilled out of my eyes, and it did absolutely nothing for the headache that had been nearly gone. These weren't the nice and happy tears that some heroines cried in blockbuster flicks, these were the big ugly fat tears that I hadn't known were in me.

"I-I am supposed to be a Quinn witch, but the one woman who might have told me what that meant is dead and now...now some woman pretending to be my mom is showing up in my bedroom, telling me to come talk with her and I think I have friends, real friends, and I've never had those before. My dad has been lying to me all my life, and on top of that, Alan kissed me, and Dmitri reads me stories, and you have the prettiest damn sneer I've ever seen!"

I crumpled. My legs wouldn't hold me up anymore, and I just fell down in front of Wei. Of all the people I had ever met, he was the one I wanted to look strong for, and all I could do was sob those ugly deep rib-cracking sobs that came with the gross nose and bright red cheeks.

"I don't know...what...to do," I managed to say between breaths.

I expected him to make some terrible comment, to say something rude. Imagine my surprise when he sat down behind me and pulled me against him. His body rocked, and his hand pressed my ear to his chest. Had he been human, I would have heard a heartbeat. Instead, all I felt was the caress of his shirt, stained with my tears, and the strength of the body beneath it.

All I wanted to do was curl up and fall back asleep. When had I gone from feeling like everything was alright, to feeling like nothing was? I had been on a great date tonight. I had friends. But it all felt...like it was someone else's dream. That was dumb. Maybe everything would make more sense in the morning.

He didn't say anything. He didn't tell me that it would be alright, and he didn't say that I shouldn't be crying. Wei just held me close and rocked me until the need to cry finally ebbed.

"What do you mean when you say that your mother visited you?"

"I don't know that it was her. I'm not sure I believe it. But some woman in a gray robe has visited me twice, once at Ms. Marquesa's store, and once in my bedroom before I came out here. She says she is my mother and that she wants to talk to me about the prophecy."

I made to pull away, and he let me, though his hands lingered on my arms longer than I thought they would. Maybe he didn't hate me as much as I thought he did.

"Will you go to her?"

"Hell no," I said flatly. "I don't know who she is or what she wants from me. I've seen enough movies to know how that kind of thing goes. She's either my mother and has known who and what I am this whole time and left me anyway, or she's not my mother and she's trying to lure me into a trap. Either way, I am not interested."

"That is...somehow wise."

"You sound awfully surprised by that."

He pulled back an inch, which only told me that he had been too close to start with. "Maybe I am." He stood up and bowed to me again. I almost bowed back, but I was too sure that I'd screw it up to try. "Will you be able to sleep now?"

I thought about it and shook my head. "I am way too awake for that."

"Would you like me to stay?" he asked. I think he even meant it.

117

I couldn't help but wonder who Wei really was. I wasn't stupid enough to think that he wasn't as powerful or as deadly as he seemed. I was pretty sure he was both. But I also wasn't stupid enough to think that was all he was.

"What kind of sword is that?" I asked, pointing to the straight blade with the tassel.

"It's a jian, a sword used in Tai Chi."

I had heard of Tai Chi. I knew that it was Chinese in origin, and that was pretty much all. I hadn't known that there were swords involved.

"Could you teach me how to use it?" I asked.

"Why?"

"Dude, I have spent at least a third of my life running around a digital daydream pretending to be a hero. If I have the chance to learn to use a sword, I'm going to take a shot."

His lips split into a grin that made his face appear softer. *He was cute*, I thought. He might not have the overt sensuality of Alan, or the warrior-poet beauty of Dmitri...but there was something beautiful about him nonetheless. I wondered if they were beautiful because they were vampires, or if they had to be beautiful before someone would change them.

"It will not be easy."

"The best things in life never are."

CHAPTER ELEVEN

"Ugh, I can't do this."

I tossed an old fashioned feathered pen on the ground; it rolled next to a vial of bright blue ink. I was not, apparently, an ink witch; nor was I a witch of fire, earth, air, or any one of the other elements. I was not good with yarn or thread or other forms of stitch-witchery. I wasn't a kitchen witch, or an herbalist, a beast witch, or anything else, so far as I could tell.

"Maybe I'm not really a witch. Maybe I just kinda suck at all of this."

"That is a terrible attitude to have," Ms. Marquesa said shortly. I couldn't really blame her for getting snippy with me. I'd been snippy for the past month at least. I hadn't really slept well since the night my maybe-mom had shown up to surprise me. I was filling my time with training, both arcane and martial. The Tai Chi was all about muscle control and fluid movement, and dear sweet merciful gods of gaming, it made everything hurt. My arms were starting to look fantastic, though, so there was that. I hadn't been allowed to use a sword yet.

The arcane stuff was going a lot...slower.

"Yer heart just ain't in this." Ms. Marquesa waved her hands. The herbal smoke that had gathered between her palms evaporated, taking the scent of rosemary and bay leaves with it. She looked, in my opinion, exactly how a witch ought to look. She wore layered, loose colors that might have been sheer were it not for the stacking and a few talismans around her neck with symbols that I was beginning to recognize as moon glyphs.

"Well, I don't know where it would be," I grumped, tugging at my college sweater. I didn't look nearly as witchy. In fact, I looked like a college student in the middle of the worst round of finals she had ever known. I kinda felt that way, too. Go figure.

"Boys," Connie said. She held out one hand and the squirrel who had come to her while the four of us; Ms. Marquesa, Connie, Jenny, and myself; had gathered at Ms. Marquesa's place to practice magic. She lived in an old three-bedroom house. It was everything that my grandma's house hadn't been, neat and organized and full of food. As Ms. Marquesa was a kitchen witch, I didn't know why I expected any less.

I shot Connie a look. It was true, but she didn't have to say it. Boys were on my mind, a lot. Ever since I started training with Wei, Dmitri and Alan had decided to step up how much attention they were giving me. It sounded great, in theory, to have the attention of three very attractive immortal dudes, but I had spent a good portion of my life not being around people a lot. It was beginning to grate on my nerves.

Jenny laughed, stretched out her legging-clad legs, and flopped backwards on a bean bag. The bright red of it brought out the gold shadow she'd smeared over her eyelids. I'd learned that she never bought anything that wasn't drug store brand or thrift store-centric, and yet she always managed to look like she'd just stepped off a runway. She never failed to impress. "I wish I had three hot vampire chicks to date."

I wished she did, too, and I said so. She shot me a friendly smirk but I couldn't help but notice the way her eyes lingered on Connie.

I wished Connie was gay, but as far as I could tell, she wasn't interested in dating at all, no matter the gender. Or maybe she just wasn't interested in vampires, since those were the only boys I currently knew.

 It had been decided that, while me learning magic was absolutely necessary, it was not necessary for me to put myself in a place where my maybe-mom might be able to visit without someone there to protect me. I'd been able to stop them from hanging around in my bedroom at night, but I hadn't been able to stop them from escorting me home from lessons. Alan would always show up a little early so that he could flirt and chat. That boy loved being the center of attention. Connie pretty much ignored him.

I mean, I had met people who didn't like romance or sex. They were few and far between, but they existed and were, for the most part, some of the coolest people I had known. Maybe Connie was one of them. I didn't know, and I didn't want to ask out of fear of being creepy, or rude. How do you say 'excuse me, but I couldn't help you not noticing the googly eyes that Jenny tosses in your direction, are you straight or just not interested in hot people' without sounding like a complete idiot? Answer: you don't.

"It sounds great," I said with a roll of my shoulders. "It's not."

It was getting less and less great every day. The boys, as I called them despite the fact that they were all older than me by a couple centuries each, bickered. Oh, it started over trivial things like who took whose vial of blood from the fridge, or who moved whose current hobby or work-related task from where it had been left. No one would fess up, everyone would grump, and even I could see that it was getting worse.

"You need to choose," Jenny said gently.

"I don't love any of them."

No one had anything to say about that. I had even really committed myself completely to this whole prophecy anyway. There was still a pretty big part of me that was sure I'd be leaving after these few months and going back to my fast food lifestyle...you know, after I learned some magic.

"Don'cha think about that now," Ms. Marquesa's voice carried across my moody thoughts. "We are practicin'. Get yer head in this, girl, or you ain't ev'a gonna learn."

She was right, and I knew it. I was just frustrated. I had tried what felt like everything, and nothing was clicking with me. Everyone was telling me that it was okay, some witches found their niche later than others, and that I could work on other things. But I couldn't seem to get my mind wrapped around this whole witchcraft thing unless I knew what was going on.

"I'm sorry, Ms. Marquesa," I said honestly.

All the sternness in her face fell away and she gave me a look that said she understood. She waved a hand away and stood up. "Alright, let's eat, let's talk, and then we will try again."

Food seemed to solve everything for Ms. Marquesa. I couldn't blame her. Food was pretty awesome. Good Ol' Pete could cook like nothing else, but it was all very fine and very elegant. I always felt like I was eating at some posh restaurant when he made food. Ms. Marquesa's cooking made me feel like I was home. She wandered over to the fridge and took out what looked to be the world's biggest piece of bacon. It was as long as a cutting board and perfectly square.

"What the heck is that?" I asked.

"Pork belly," she said, "best comfort food there ev'a was, an' right now I think that's what'cha need. An' it helps that pork is good for that sort of thing."

"Comfort?" I asked, completely intrigued. I loved learning about magic and all the magical things in the world.

"A pig is an earthy animal, and Earth is..." she trailed off, giving me a sidelong glance.

"Earth is the element of wisdom, strength, learning, and home."

"That is right from yer grandma's book," she nodded. She pulled out a knife. The wooden handle was worn to a sheen from being handled so much, but I could still see symbols for protection, health, and comfort carved into it. She cut long deep lines in the pork. "It's good information, no lie there, but'cha gotta start looking at what Earth means to you. Add on to that definition in yer head."

I frowned and thought long and hard about that. What did Earth, the element, mean to me, the witch? "It's where life starts. You put the seed in it and it...it all starts there. I mean, I know that science tells us that life started in the water, but us, our life started when what was in the water wanted to come on land. It was the big force of it all."

She smiled at me. "New beginnings, new life. That's good. You oughta put that in the book."

My eyes went wide, and she must have noticed, because she gave a great big belly laugh. "What? You thought that book was only good for readin'? Oh, honey, no. It's a grimoire; it's meant to be written in. To be edited and changed. It's yours now."

The thought had seriously never occurred to me. Books were information, evidence, and...I dunno. It felt like some weird kind of blasphemy to write in my grandmother's book. "I...I don't...think I could do that."

She sighed and pulled out a slew of herbs. I couldn't recognize all of their names, but I knew the first few were for happiness, the others were for inspiration. She put cloves, a fiery herb good for luck and friendship and romance, into a warm pan with some cinnamon; also good for warmth, prosperity and luck. She stirred them in the pan with a wooden spoon until the scent of it filled the room.

"Grandma, maybe she might do bettah with her own book," Jenny suggested.

Ms. Marquesa seemed to think that over as she stirred. When the herbs had darkened and the house was smelling amazing, she poured the contents into a big mortar and pestle. She added a few more things I couldn't see and began to slowly grind everything together. "What makes you say that?"

It wasn't a challenge, or at least, it wasn't a mean one. She was curious.

"Well, she her own person. She doesn't like others telling her what she ought to be doing, she likes deciding for herself. We both know a grimoire doesn't gotta be a big fancy book. She can just get a journal down from the drug store and start using that."

"Ain't a bad idea," Ms. Marquesa said, nodding her head before adding oil and honey to the mixture. Oil, I knew, was about binding everything together. Honey fed energy. The moment the two hit the mix, I could feel the magic really beginning. She stirred and swayed slowly back and forth as she did it. "Ain't a bad idea a'tall."

She poured the mix over the slab of pork and used her fingers to rub it in, then she tucked it in the oven.

"Well," she said, turning back to us. "Why don't you just take her on down to the store and pick up a journal for her? We'll have dinner, and then y'all can go out."

"Out?" I'm pretty sure the three of us said it in full surround sound, choir-worthy unison.

She turned towards us, putting a hand still coated in herbs on her hip, and gave us a look worthy of the ultimate stupidity. I don't think we'd earned that look, but I was still feeling kinda lost, like she'd had half of a conversation without us.

"It's Friday night, ain't it? Don't you young people go out sometimes? All of y'all are hopeless."

"We go out," Jenny said.

"Going to the movies don't count if you ain't there to flirt. In my day, on Friday nights, me and all my friends would get dressed up in our best and go down to Blackburn to party."

I couldn't picture Ms. Marquesa partying, but I also knew she didn't lie. "Blackburn?"

124

"There's like...three colleges around Blackburn," Jenny explained. "The clubs are pretty much packed on the weekends, unless it's finals week. One of them is a military college, too, so...lots of uniforms."

"Mmf," was Connie's reply. I guess she wasn't completely immune to hotness. Maybe she just didn't like Alan. I couldn't blame her. Alan's flirting wasn't for everyone.

"It's not a terrible idea," I admitted. I didn't do a lot of clubbing, but right now, loud music and dancing and virgin versions of alcoholic drinks sounded pretty much fantastic. Besides, aside from the super posh dates that Alan had been taking me on, I didn't get a chance to dress up for anything.

"Let's do it," Connie said.

Jenny grinned. I could already see her thinking about working up the courage to ask Connie to dance. If she didn't, I was going to nag her until it happened. I didn't want to be pushy, but everyone was nagging at me about my romantic life. I was going to return the favor.

"Cool!"

Dinner was, without surprise, fantastic. I realized that all the herbs that Ms. Marquesa had used were attuned to the element of fire, which was all about making decisions and being passionate. Seemed like a great idea before throwing us into a club filled with college-aged kids.

I didn't know until the doorbell rang that she'd called the boys while we'd been out picking up a journal and new outfits for the night.

It was just after nightfall, and that should have been my first clue. But I was too busy staring into the bathroom mirror trying to get my make-up to match the little black dress that I had found in the thrift store. Connie was next to me; she was ignoring most of the make-up. She'd traded her jeans for...other jeans. I wasn't surprised. I had never known her to wear anything but jeans or camo. But the tank top she had picked out had some sparkle around the neckline. It showed off her super adorable freckles. Her hair was tugged back at the sides, making her unruly curls look slightly less unruly. I could see part of why Jenny liked her. She could be cute.

Jenny, like always, looked like she just got back from Milan. Her skirt was a fringe across her mahogany thighs and the loose top she wore was just sheer enough that I could see the lines of her bra. On another girl, it might have looked slutty, but she managed to make it look like grade A class. Her lips were as red as her shoes and the wide belt that she wore.

"Who is that?" I asked, trying to peek out the bathroom door.

"Guess," Connie said, smearing lip gloss, her only make-up, on.

I frowned, and then I heard the charming laugh of one Alan Pierre Rouergue, of the House of Rouergue.

"It's not Alan's night to pick me up," I said, even though I had sent a text to Peter to let him know that I would be hanging out with the girls this evening and that I wouldn't need an escort home. Then, I heard the tell-tale rumble of Dmitri and knew that something was wrong.

Of all the in-fighting that had been going on, what happened between Dmitri and Alan was the worst. Alan was usually to blame. He'd make some little comment about our last date, and Dmitri would glower. Alan would make another comment, and before I knew it, they were at each other's throats. This could not be good.

"Shit," I cursed, and stepped out of the bathroom. I was planning the tongue lashing I was about to bestow when I stopped dead halfway there. It wasn't just Alan and Dmitri; Wei was there, too, and they all looked...hot. Like, okay, they always looked good, but tonight was completely different. Usually Alan was wearing something mid-18th century, and Dmitri was always in black, and Wei liked his Chinese martial arts uniforms...but tonight, they could have been human...really hot humans.

Dmitri was wearing black slacks, sure, but the red button down shirt he wore and the open vest made his uniform of angst into sleek fashion. Alan had left the frilly shirts at home and, instead, wore tailored khaki's and a dark green collared shirt that made his sapphire eyes seem to glow. He'd even braided his hair. Wei was wearing jeans. Honest to god jeans and a simple white cotton shirt beneath a leather jacket. Were it not for his long sweep of black hair, he might have looked like a greaser from the fifties.

"Holy crap," I said. "What are you guys doing here?"

"*Ma cher,* you look fantastic." Alan's eyes swept over me in a way that I could only call hungry. I flushed.

"Thanks, but that doesn't answer my question."

"We are here to escort you to the...parties," Dmitri answered.

"Oh, no you aren't." There was absolutely nothing good that could come from letting loose three hot vampires in a nightclub with a bunch of stressed out and horny college students. Add in two witches and a potential prophecy girl? No, I knew how that chapter was going to go. Not good.

"Yes." Wei's answer was simple and did not leave a whole lot of room for argument. His golden thumbs hooked in the dark denim of his belt loops, and he fixed me with a look that said "don't bother to argue."

"No, you aren't." I had never been good at listening. "This is a bad idea, a terrible idea."

"What's going on?" Jenny came out of the bathroom, managing to make a strut in four-inch heels look smooth.

"They say they are going with us." I motioned wildly at the vampire boy band lined up behind me.

"Oh. Cool."

"Cool?" I asked, hardly believing what Jenny had said.

She shrugged one shoulder. "What better way to deal with idiots that we don't want to deal with than having a vampire or two in our corner? Besides, they look ready to go."

I opened and closed my mouth several times before I managed to say, "You're serious?"

"Do you wanna stand here and argue, *ma cher*? Or do you wish to go?"

I grabbed my jacket off the hanger. "This is a terrible idea. I'm saying this now so that when I say 'I told you so' later, you all know what I am talking about."

CHAPTER 12

To be fair, it all started off fantastic. We didn't have to wait. The bouncer took one look at us, walking up in all of our glory, and decided that we were cool enough to go in. I didn't even have to pay cover. It was a first for me.

The club was nicer than I expected, three stories tall with a dance floor taking up the entire bottom half. The second floor was a bar with drinks and the third was VIP, with its own private dance space. I don't know how we got there, but we ended up in the VIP lounge with drinks pressed into our hands. No one even ID'ed us, which I thought was pretty lax on the club's part.

"I'm gonna go dance," Connie said before she had even taken a sip of her drink.

"I'll go with you." Jenny jumped up.

"And I will not allow two lovely mademoiselles to go down there without an escort." Alan bowed gracefully and took them each by the hand. I watched the trio laugh and descend down the stairs that we had just come up to join the throng of the crowd below. It was only nine o'clock, so the throng was pretty small for the moment, but even so, the three of them made a splash. People, myself included, watched as they moved onto the dance floor and continued to watch when they started to dance. They were good.

"Do you dance?" Dmitri leaned over and asked me. The music was loud enough that I had to lean close to hear him. I didn't have supernatural ears.

I shook my head. "Not unless I've just beaten a boss level."

He smiled. I'd been teaching him the joy of video games. He wasn't too bad. He still preferred books, and I couldn't blame him for that.

"Will you dance with me?"

He sounded so unsure of himself when he asked. His big warm eyes were focused on some invisible piece of lint on his slacks.

"Maybe after a drink or two."

Admittedly, none of the drinks I was drinking had any liquid confidence in them, but I kinda wanted to wait until the dance floor had a few more people. This way, if I made a complete fool of myself, it would be masked by the slew of other people being foolish.

I sat back, and he put his arm around my shoulders. He was muscular enough that it was a little uncomfortable, but I didn't want to make him feel bad for having an excellent body, so I stayed there.

"How did the lesson go?" he asked.

I frowned. "The same as usual. Everyone but me was awesome."

"You worry too much," Wei cut in. I hadn't actually expected him to speak. I assumed that he'd just stand there, looking like a body guard. He'd taken off the jacket. It should have made him look less intimidating. It didn't. His long, loose hair was a curtain around his face. "You think too much about how good others are. You seem to believe if you are not perfect in the beginning, you should move on. Some things take time."

I blinked. It was pretty much a speech as far as Wei was concerned. He'd talked to me more since we had started our lessons in Tai Chi, but not a whole lot more. Usually just instructions on how to move my feet and what I ought to be visualizing.

Dmitri sighed. "He is right." I could tell he didn't like saying it.

"Oh...good," I said, feeling a little bit pissed off. I hadn't come out tonight to be told about my numerous flaws. I'd come out to relax and have fun and look cute doing it. So far, I had succeeded in the last, and nothing else. I sighed and moved away from Dmitri, no longer wanting to lounge against him.

He looked hurt. I hated that I had made him feel that way, but my feelings mattered, too. "Here's a rule for tonight," I snapped, feeling a little grumpy, "Tonight, we aren't going to talk about my weaknesses, the prophecy, babies, or how I'm doing in magic. I'd prefer if we didn't talk about me at all."

Wei raised his brow at me. "If that's your wish."

I knew when he said it that he meant it. Wei didn't say anything unless he meant it. The fact that he didn't argue, make any demands, or try to reason with my request meant a lot to me right then. I realized that I could always count on Wei, and that made me love him just a little bit.

Shit.

"Why?" Dmitri wanted to know. He was looking a little peeved. Great. Wei got it. He didn't need to understand why. He just needed to know what I needed and that was that. Could Dmitri just let it go? Nope. He had to know why I wanted something, and then he'd pick it apart. I could already feel it happening.

"Because I just want to relax," I explained. "My whole life this past...jeez, has it already been five weeks?...my whole life recently has consisted of being bad at magic and being bad at dating without a whole lot in between."

"Your work in Tai Chi has been commendable."

I blinked in surprise. "Thank you."

Wei bowed. Dmitri glowered. He'd been glowering a lot lately. I was quickly getting fed up with it.

"Has dating me been bad?" he wanted to know.

I took a long drink from something that tasted like cherries and pineapple. It should have tasted amazing, considering those were two of my favorite flavors, but I could barely enjoy it. "No, dating you has not been bad. Dating you would be fantastic if you weren't so...difficult."

I hated to say it, but it was true.

"How is it difficult?" he demanded.

I waved a hand between us. "This, this is how it is difficult. This, right here. Dude, listen, you are so cute, and so creative, and I love the way you read books, but the moment that something isn't exactly how you'd like it to be, you just get grumpy. You make it about how you are feeling right then and forget that other people are having feelings, too. You want me to dance with you. You want me to cuddle with you. I get it. But dammit..." I huffed as the rain of anger I'd been riding derailed and all of my words just sort of disappeared in a rush of frustration. "You can be so...difficult."

"And you want easy," he snapped.

Alan chose that exact moment to walk up the stairs. Great. If ever there was the definition of easy...there it was. Dmitri sneered at Alan. Alan raised one perfect brow.

"What did I do?" he wanted to know.

"You exist."

Dmitri surged to his feet and stormed off. Alan watched him go. I sighed.

"Well, that...was unexpected," Alan said. He picked up one of the myriad of drinks that still sat on the see-through table and took a long sip. "What's gotten under our prickly boy's skin?"

"You," Wei said without any anger. "He sees that Lorena is not falling in love with him, and he blames you."

"You are breaking the rules," I said.

He bowed his head. "True. My apologies."

"Rules?" Alan asked, taking another sip of drink.

"Lorena does not wish to talk about the prophecy or her flaws tonight. I believe she just wants to have fun."

"That's all girls really want," I said, parodying the song. I don't think they got it. Woe is me to only be funny to the people who get mid-80's pop references.

Wei stood up. "I am going to find Dmitri and make sure that he does not reveal us to the humans." And just like that, he was gone. He moved fast, faster than Dmitri or Alan. One moment, he could be there, the next he could be gone. I'd gotten used to vampire movement, the way they could just...swoosh...like super heroes. Wei was The Flash, the other two were Superman, and yeah...The Flash was faster.

"I hate to break the rules, but is it true?" Alan asked.

"Is what true?" I said, realizing that I wouldn't be able to get to have fun until we had a whole conversation about me and the prophecy.

"Do you not love Dmitri?"

I sighed and dragged a hand through my hair. "I should, right? He's cute, and he's strong, and he reads and write and paints. Have you seen his paintings? They are gorgeous. And he leaves me these little sketches and love notes and everything..."

"And yet..." Alan asked, prompting me to go on.

"And yet...I don't love him. I'm attracted to him. I think he'd look great naked, and I could listen to him read sonnets for the rest of my life but...every time I talk to him, I always have to be worried about what I might say. He can be so damn...moody."

Alan laughed, but there was a sparkle in his eye. I finally said what I'd been waiting to say for like...a month.

"It would help if you weren't totally in love with him."

The laugh cut off. He gave me a look. "I beg your pardon?"

I sighed, rubbing my fingers across my forehead. "I moved around a lot in high school. I've told you that before. While I hated all the moving, I got to learn a lot about people. How the people who are in Alaska are pretty much the same as the ones in Florida, despite the huge difference in cultures."

"Both of those places are American."

I shrugged. "That's true, but that doesn't make them the same. Anthropology was my major, so bear with me if I zone off and explain the cultural differences between places whose only common denominator is the language they speak and the government they pay taxes to."

He smiled at me. "So, you think I am in love with Dmitri."

"I know you are. I think you have been for a long time. You poke at him, you prod at him, and you do it so he will pay attention to you. I've watched you do it. When you think he is giving me just a little too much attention, you'll sneak some little offhand remark in there that you know is going to bug him."

He swirled his drink in his cup. His face had taken on that neutral, but mildly amused, face that I knew meant he was hiding something. "I could be trying to get your attention."

I nodded. "You could, but I know better. You aim the comments at him, knowing that he's going to flip out. You aren't trying to get my attention, you are trying to get his. You love him."

134

He sighed and set down his cup. "I assume this takes me out of the running."

I looked at him. His long braid had swept over his shoulder, looking like a golden rope. I reached out and ran my fingers over it. It was as soft as it looked. "I don't know what it does. I can honestly say that I hate the idea that I know when you are kissing me, a part of you is thinking about him."

"I like kissing you, Lorena."

He didn't call me by my pet name, and it hurt just a little. "I know," I said, "but you don't love me any more than I love you."

He snorted, but he didn't disagree with me. "For a human, you are wise."

"For a vampire, you're just plain pretty."

He laughed and opened his arms. I slid over to them, felt them wrap around me. He was hugging me goodbye, and we both knew it. He felt good, really good. He probably would have been a lot of fun to sleep with, but what was between us wasn't love, and it never would be. Too bad. I'd never gotten to see him naked.

He placed his crooked finger beneath my chin, and I lifted my head to gaze into those lovely eyes.

"When you finally do fall in love with Dmitri, treat him well, won't you?"

The mask slipped away completely, and I could see the warm hope in his eyes. The silent begging that I wouldn't hurt the man that he loved. I nodded, swallowing the knot that had formed in my throat. He dipped his head and placed the chastest kiss on my lips that I had ever felt. It was a soft kiss, a thank you kiss, and it was just that moment that Dmitri decided to come back.

"So we cannot talk about romance, but he can kiss you?"

I jerked away suddenly. Alan didn't. It was that moment that I knew that Alan had heard Dmitri coming. He had used the situation to his advantage. I wanted to be mad at him. Okay, I was a little mad at him, but after seeing all that raw emotion in his eyes, I couldn't really hold it against him. He was in love, and there was nothing he could do about it.

"Dmitri, wait." I held up one hand. I opened my mouth to explain, but what was I supposed to say? That Alan had just admitted to me that he wasn't going to pursue me because he was too in love with Dmitri? Yeah, that didn't really feel like my secret to tell.

"Dmitri," Alan stood up and bowed. "Lorena was just saying goodbye. She has...ended...my courting of her. You've won."

I shot Alan a look. That wasn't fair. I hadn't decided on anything. Just because I wasn't going to be seeing Alan romantically anymore didn't mean I was going to jump into bed with Dmitri. I still didn't love him, and I didn't know if I ever would. I hated a guy I had to tiptoe around.

"Is this true?" Wei asked.

"Kinda," I answered.

Dmitri's eyes lit up. He closed the space between us in a blur of speed that just barely stayed inside the realm of human ability, even though it still caused a few heads to turn. His big strong arms were around me. "Really?"

I put my hands on his biceps. They were firm and hard beneath my hands. I swallowed. "Don't get too excited. Just because I broke the romance off with him doesn't mean I'm ready to be the prophecy girl."

The light in his eyes dimmed. I could see that he wanted to ask the why, the how, the what. He wanted to question my decision. But he swallowed it. "I'll wait as long as you need."

No, he wouldn't. I knew that looking into his face, surrounded by all those curls. He'd wait a while, maybe even longer than I thought he would, but sooner or later he'd make demands. He'd question.

"Will you dance with me?" he asked softly.

I didn't really want to, but I couldn't bring myself to say no and kill what little hope he had. I nodded, and he took my hand in his and led me onto the dance floor.

The song wasn't quite slow, but it wasn't fast either. There was a techno beat to it, like the rhythm of the heart. His hands went to my hips, and I began to move.

I am not the world's best dancer. I move with more enthusiasm than skill, but I love the way dancing feels. I love the way my body finds a rhythm and moves with it. I like how professionals can make a song into a story, using their bodies to tell it. I wasn't one of those. My only dance classes had been six after-school classes at the Y. Even so, it was easy to move back and forth with Dmitri's hands on my hips.

He was smiling at me, grinning as if he had just won some great competition. Well, I thought to myself, he was pretty sure he had. He stepped forward and matched his movements to my own, his fingers possessive on my hips.

Had he won? I wondered. There wasn't anyone else to choose. Then again, I didn't really have to choose, did I? I could still go home or to whatever I called home. Sure, having my grandmother's house and all the money from her estate would be fantastic...but not ultimately necessary. I had half a college degree in a field that no one had heard of and many years in the wild world of fast food customer service. What did I have to worry about?

And then there was the fact that I knew that if I didn't take part in this prophecy, if I didn't choose one of the Sons of Vlad and have a baby...I was dooming magic to die. Damn. I really did not want magic to die. I wanted...well, I wanted magic to thrive. I wanted to see mermaids taking selfies and dragons guarding banks and who knew what else.

And all I had to do was fall in love with Dmitri, right? Well, no. I didn't *have* to. I could just take him to bed. There were worse things in the world than enjoying the body of a super-hot paranormal dude, but the truth was, I wasn't sure I would enjoy it unless I really, really felt something for him...and I ought to enjoy it, right?

Right.

So, what was there left to do but fall in love with my moody vampire? I glanced past his shoulder and saw Wei.

He was sitting on a bar stool, watching with eyes as cool and calm as a cat's. His lips were set into that perfectly neutral line that he could conjure up. He caught me watching him, and he bowed his head ever so slightly so that his hair fell over his face. My heart did a little skip. What the hell was that about?

Oh no.

I blinked and turned my attention back to Dmitri who was still smiling at me like I was everything in the world. Oh no. He slid his arms even tighter around me and pulled me closer as the music took it down another notch. The lights were low and there were sparkles on the walls as twenty or so other couples stepped into the embrace of their partners' arms.

"Are you alright?" Dmitri asked.

"Nervous," I said. It was true. I was nervous. This felt heavy. I'd spent a lot of time with Dmitri and Alan before now, but tonight felt...different.

He lifted a hand to my cheek. "Don't be."

He kissed me before I realized what he was going to do. I damn near froze. The kiss was good. My body tingled, hummed, to be so close to a cute guy, but even so, a single thought hit me.

"Where's Jenny?" I asked.

Dmitri jerked as if he'd been struck. He looked confused and a little hurt. I couldn't blame him. I'd just ruined our first kiss by wondering about my friend. But even so, my eyes darted around the dance floor. I couldn't see Jenny anywhere, but there was Connie with her head pressed to some uniformed college boy's chest. Oh no.

Dmitri followed the line of my gaze. He frowned, but he didn't release me.

"She's around."

I frowned at him. "Yeah, but I'm going to go find her."

"Why?" he wanted to know.

That irked me. "Dude, if you don't understand why I'm going to go look for Jenny, then I can't help you."

I turned and walked off the dance floor, leaving a confused and grumpy guy behind me. The first place I checked was the women's room. It's where I would go if the person I'd been crushing on was slow-dancing with someone else. There was no better place to cry. But the line was about a trillion girls long, and I didn't know if I could wait that long to find her.

"What is it?" Wei asked.

"I can't find Jenny."

He raised his brow, but didn't question it. "What can I do?"

"I don't know enough about vampire abilities to answer that question. Can you like...feel her?"

He shook his head. He didn't make fun of me for asking. I liked that. "No, and there are too many people here to sense her heartbeat."

I filed that bit of information away for later. "I don't know what to do."

He looked at me, his eyes, like flecks of obsidian, were warm with some emotion I couldn't name. "You are a witch."

"A terrible one."

He grabbed my shoulders suddenly in his hands and made me look at him. "I do not want to hear those words again."

"I...what?'

He didn't shake me like I expected him to. Instead, his fingers dug in just enough that I could feel the steady iron-like pressure of them. "You tell yourself that you are bad, and you leave yourself no room to improve. I have felt your talent. Stop it."

He meant it. Wei never said anything that he didn't mean.

"What do you mean you felt it?"

"The day you broke the window."

I thought back to it. I remembered all the lines, the grand inter-connectivity of the Weave. Could that help me now? "You felt that?"

He nodded. "Find her."

"I need some place a little less...loud."

He nodded and wrapped his arms around me. For the second time that night, my heart skipped a beat. What was wrong with me? I decided not to think about that, not right now. I felt a surge of motion, and the next thing I knew, we were in a basement. The boxes of liquor were enough to tell me we were still in the club, just kind of below it.

"What can I do?"

"Just...stay," I answered.

I would have told Dmitri to back up, or Alan to be quiet. Wei, I knew, wouldn't do anything unless I asked it of him or unless I was in danger. Damn. I didn't want to like him. He was grumpy.

I took a deep breath and closed my eyes. Through the concrete floor, I could hear the music still pounding away, the thump-thrum heartbeat of it. Rather than ignore it, I focused on it, waiting for my own heartbeat, which was a little unsteady, to match it. I slowed my breathing down.

The trick to meditation, I had learned, wasn't to try to clear my head. It was to let all the thoughts I had go without dwelling on them. Did I want to think about my unexpected feelings for Wei? Nope, absolutely not. Did I want to think about the way Dmitri looked at me? Negative. Hard pass. Or Alan, who was pretty much destined to be stuck in Dmitri's not-even-a-friend zone? Not even a little. All I wanted to do was focus on Jenny and find her.

My breathing slowed down to almost nothing, my chest barely rose and fell inside of my awesome little black dress. I was aware of the way my feet felt in my sandals, of the quiet ocean that was Wei on my left. Then, I felt the dance floor, the people and their hundreds of emotions flying through them. I felt the anxiety of servers, the lust and fever of horny college kids. The stress and the hope and the depression and the dreams and aspirations of all of them curled over one another in some grand miasma of humanity.

"I...I can't...it's too much."

Cool fingers touched my chin, and my skin seemed to flare to life. When I opened my eyes, I could see Wei's face, rounded with his Asian features, and then I didn't see him. I saw the power of him. It was this well of energy that didn't really have a color. But I could have dipped my hands into it if I'd wanted to. I reached for it instead, brushing my fingers through it. Energy jumped into my grasp.

He made a sound, and it was not an unpleasant one. I wanted to hear it again. I stroked that source of power once more and Wei hissed. "What are you doing?"

"I....don't...know."

It felt so good, that power source. It jumped to my fingers and swam against my skin. I opened my eyes, and I could see everyone in the club. I mean, I couldn't see their faces, but I felt their energy, their souls, their lives, whatever you wanted to call it. Everyone had this little ball of energy tucked inside of them. Some were brighter than others, some were even color-coded for my convenience.

A particularly angry guy was bright red, mixed with black, the dude to his left had a blue sphere of life, tinged with bile green. That didn't seem like a good pair. A moment later, they started to fight. A bouncer whose energy was a bright vibrant orange grabbed them both and tossed them out. I didn't know what it all meant, but I knew that this wasn't normal...that this was all me.

I didn't dwell on it. I didn't want to understand just yet. Instead, I searched through one aura after another until I found Jenny. She was outside, tucked between the club and the closed bookstore next door. She was holding herself, and her own ball of energy was so dark blue that it was almost black.

"I know where she is."

I broke out of the meditation suddenly. I was surprised to find that my hand was on Wei's chest. His eyes were wide, his lips were parted, and he looked as if I had just sucked the life out of him.

"Wei? What's wrong?"

"Well," Alan said, "you found your source."

I jumped. I hadn't realized that he would be there. "My...source? What? I mean...I know what a source is but..."

Wei pulled back, but he was unsteady on his feet. "It would make sense."

Alan nodded. "It would."

"Enough with the vagueness," I said, stepping away from both of them. "What happened?"

Wei shook his head. "Do not worry about it now. I saw what you saw. Go to Jenny. We will discuss it later."

I frowned at him. I didn't want to discuss it later, but I knew that understanding what had just happened wasn't nearly as important as getting to Jenny. I looked at Alan.

"Go. I will see that he feeds."

"Feeds?" I asked. Jeez, what the hell had I done?

"You took some of his magic and made it yours, Lorena. Go, I will tend to him."

I took Alan at his word and headed upstairs, ignoring the looks from the kitchen staff as I did. I didn't hear them demand to know what I was doing. All I heard were Alan's words telling me that I had taken some of Wei's magic. How had I done that? I didn't think it was possible. No, I thought, I knew that it wasn't possible. One of my grandmother's books had made that really clear. The only thing that could steal power from another person were a few particular types of faeries and one very specific kind of vampire that, according to the boys, didn't exist anymore.

So what had I done...and why had it felt so good?

CHAPTER 13

When I got to Jenny, she didn't look like she'd stepped off a runway. She looked like she'd just had the worst prom ever. She was sitting on the ground in her cute outfit, trying to hide the fact that she had been crying.

"Hey," I said.

She didn't look at me. "Hey."

I said a silent prayer of forgiveness to my dress and plopped down next to her. I didn't say anything. I just opened my arms for a hug. She plopped against me, a pile of human misery.

"You okay?" I asked. It was a stupid question, but I couldn't think of what else to say.

"Yeah...why wouldn't I be?" She tried to smile at me, but it didn't quite reach her eyes.

"Because your crush is totally going on a date with some dude tonight."

She didn't say anything at first. She just sat there with her head pillowed on my shoulder as more tears ran down her cheeks. These ones she didn't bother to hide.

"I shouldn't care," she finally said. "She's never given me any reason to think that she was into me. We've just been friends. I'm not some jackass who is only nice to girls so that they'll date me."

"I know that," I said.

"I shouldn't care," she repeated.

"But you do."

She sat back so suddenly the ground shifted beneath us. It was impressive since she couldn't have weighed more than a hundred and ten pounds. Then again, we were sitting on concrete, which was a bunch of smashed up rock, and Jenny was all about the power of rocks. "I do. I do care, and it's stupid."

"It's not stupid."

She gave a snort that told me just how little she agreed with me. I gave her another hug and said again, "It's not stupid. You can't help who you like. It doesn't matter if they are everything you are sure you wouldn't like...stuff just seems to happen that way."

I didn't know who I was talking to, her or me. I didn't want to dwell on it either, no matter how many times those thoughts popped into my head.

"What am I going to do?" she asked.

"Well, tonight, we are going to go back in there, we are going to dance, and when we can't feel our legs anymore, we are going to go stop at the shop and buy a zillion bags of goodies and go back to my grandmother's house and play video games, okay?"

"Why your grandmother's place?"

"Because I need some space from the guys."

"What happened?"

We were breaking the 'let's not talk about Lorena' rules for the countless time that night, but it was okay. Jenny was feeling heartbroken, and I hadn't told her the rules anyway. "Alan and I broke it off."

"Oh," she said, "so you're with Dmitri?"

"Nope," I said.

"I'm confused."

I nodded. "So am I. It's why I need the space. But first...let's dance."

She laughed, and I was grateful for it. I stood up, swiped off my dress, and offered her my hand. She took it and frowned. "Woman, what did you do?"

"We can talk about that when we get back to my grandmother's house."

A moment later, the world exploded. Magic slammed so hard on me that I literally fell to the ground. Jenny was right next to me. I rolled over, and there my maybe-mother stood. Not just a flickering, bad-stream image of her, but the real one. She wasn't wearing the robe, but her dress was the same color gray that it had been.

Power flowed off of her in waves. Not just a little power, but wells of it. I could taste it like ozone on my teeth.

"It's time to talk."

I shook my head. I had no desire to talk to someone who scared the daylights out of me. My finely-tuned sense of survival told me to run. I listened. I grabbed Jenny's hand, and we scrambled away. We got maybe five feet away before power slammed around us again. It hit me so hard that I bit my tongue. The taste of blood was thick in my mouth.

"I wanted to be gentle about this, Lorena, but tonight was too close. We are leaving."

Well, even if she wasn't my mom, she totally had the mom voice down. Guess that meant I got to be the angsty teenager.

"No, thanks."

Yeah...close enough.

I took Jenny's hand in mine again. I had every desire to run, but magic spilled over me with a strength that I could only call titanic. My head spun, and I made the smallest movement to get further away, but my body just wouldn't cooperate.

I stood up. Well, I didn't, but my body did. It was the strangest feeling. I wasn't telling my body to move, but it was doing it anyway. I dropped Jenny's hand, and I just started walking towards my mom. I should have looked weird, like some kind of ragdoll, but I didn't. I strutted...which was weird enough, because I didn't know how to strut, but that's what I did.

I moved with an effortless grace that I didn't have and followed my mom to a car I hadn't known before. I wanted to look back at Jenny to see why she wasn't calling after me, but my head wouldn't turn that way. All I did was get into a shiny black SUV and buckle in.

A moment later, my mom got into the driver's side and we were off.

I wanted to ask a hundred questions, but my mouth was acting the exact same as my body. I did not like this feeling. I felt...trapped...locked inside of my own skin. No, not even in my skin. That wasn't mine anymore. I was trapped in the very depths of my soul.

"Don't bother trying to move," my mom said. "It won't work. I have you."

I didn't like the way she said that. It was creepy, beyond creepy. My eyes, fixed on the road in front of me, watched as the pseudo-metropolitan city of Blackburn, Virginia disappeared behind us. She navigated the SUV through the curving mountain roads with ease.

"A necromancer," she scoffed. "Of all the things, my daughter could have been...she's a necromancer."

I had played enough video games to know that a necromancer was a wizard with power over the dead. What that meant and why varied from one game to the next. I just didn't know what that had to do with me. Is that what had happened earlier? Had I drawn my power from Wei who, despite his mostly animated appearance, was a dead body? Is that why he had looked so sick?

My mom didn't sound happy with the idea. I didn't know why it bothered her, but it made me feel a little uncomfortable.

"I wanted to come get to you before this. Hell, I'd tried a hundred times to find you, but oh no. Your dad just kept moving you around. As soon as I showed up in one town, I'd find out that you had left just a few days before."

If I would have had control over my own body, I would have blinked. As it was, my eyes were drying out. It kind of hurt.

"He must still have one of Loretta's looking glasses," she muttered to herself. "Damn that witch. Damn her."

That seemed unfair. I didn't really know my grandmother, but everything that I had read and heard about her so far hadn't led me to think that she was a bad person.

"I should have run away the day I knew I was pregnant with you. Oh sure, everyone thinks your grandmother is the one who spoke the prophecy. Perfect Loretta Quinn, perfect little witch of the mountains. They all waited on her hand and foot."

Who had waited on my grandmother, I wanted to ask, but my mouth was still clamped shut. The more I tried to move, the more rigid it felt.

"But I knew. I knew. I had the dream first. I saw you give birth to magic. I saw it!"

Okay...maybe my dad had taken me away because my mom was friggin' nuts. Not like the "I need medication because my brain won't let me feel happy" kind of nuts, not even the "I hear voices so I have to live in the special ward of the hospital" kind of nuts either. She was beginning to sound obsessive to the point of disquieting.

149

"I saw it first. I saw it all. But no. I was stupid. I thought I loved your father. I thought he loved me. I was stupid. Fucking stupid. He was just another boy. I should have killed him when I had the chance."

Okay, now I really wanted out of the car. My dad and I might not get along, but I didn't want him dead. Also, I totally believed she would do it.

"Stop struggling!" my mom said.

She snapped her fingers, and suddenly I had control of some of myself back. I could blink. I could breathe on my own, and I had autonomy over my own voice. Well, that was something.

"Where are we going!?" I demanded, trying not to let my voice be a terrified squeak. I almost succeeded.

"We are going to the temple."

That sounded far more ominous than it should have. Temple should have sounded more like sanctuary and less like hell-prison. Then again, I was pretty sure that nothing coming out of my mom's mouth was going to be sounding like sanctuary.

"What is that?"

"It's where I live; we all live there."

Okay, that wasn't helping anything.

"What's a necromancer?" I demanded.

"My god, he really taught you nothing. He taught you absolutely nothing and then expected you to take part in his mother's version of this prophecy? That sounds just like him."

That wasn't entirely accurate, but I got the feeling that letting her rant was the best possible thing that I could do. She sounded mad, and not just angry but the old definition of mad.

"A necromancer," she spat the word like it was gross. "is someone who bonds with the undead. They can command them, control them, steal power from them, and give power to them. If they are talented enough, they can even rip the souls from living people."

Oh. That sounded...well...intimidating.

"They are disgusting."

Well, that was just rude. I wasn't disgusting. I also wasn't sure that I was a necromancer. Then again...maybe it wasn't so crazy. It would explain what happened with Wei. Maybe it also solved the 'how do I make a kid with the undead guy" question, too.

"What are you?" I asked.

She sat up in her seat. Her shoulders squared. She stuck her nose just a little in the air. "I'm an enchantress."

Now that was a word I knew. It even had a whole section in my grandmother's famous book. An enchantress, or enchanter if you were a dude, was a witch who could use magic to manipulate a person, not just their mind, but their bodies, too. Huh, my mom thought someone who could take over a living person's head was totally cool, but a person who could bring dead stuff to life wasn't...that seemed a little weird, but okay.

"What do you mean my grandmother's version of the prophecy?"

Her lips curled into a sneer. If feelings could kill, I would have feared for my life right then.

"Your grandmother told this cute little story about you bringing magic back by making some love child with a vampire. But oh no, that's not what I saw; that is not what I saw at all."

I was almost afraid to ask, but my mouth did it anyway. "What did you see?"

"You have a child, and that child unleashes magic on the whole world, but it's not some arcane utopia, Lorena. Magic isn't all faeries and rainbows and unicorns. Magic brings back all the things from our nightmares. It's an apocalypse."

I hadn't really thought about it that way, but it made my stomach twist up in knots.

"Can you imagine what people would do, Lorena? Can you imagine what our government would do if they saw a dragon flying in the sky?"

I could imagine it. I wasn't stupid enough to think that people were just like me. In fact, I had been to enough schools around the country to know that while there were plenty of people who liked books, comics, and video games...not everyone got as involved with them as I did. They didn't connect with the story, with the characters. They just wanted to not think about life for a while. That was cool, there was no wrong way to have fun, but I wanted to live in those worlds. But I was the minority. Not everyone wanted magic, and certainly the resurgence of it would make some people afraid.

I knew exactly what people did when they were afraid.

My mother pulled into a long driveway complete with a wrought iron gate and fancy touch-screen access codes. It asked for her name, her palm print and some series of codes that I didn't hear. A moment later, she drove us towards a house that was more fortified and complex than anything else. There were a slew of people standing out front, maybe twenty or thirty, and all of them were wearing the gray robes that I was used to my mom wearing.

That wasn't creepy at all.

When the car stopped, I just sat there. I might have had basic control over my eyes and mouth, but everything else was still under the dominion of my enchantress-mom. I was, by now, pretty sure that she was my mom. If she wasn't, she really believed that she was, and that was just as dangerous.

I stayed in the car while she approached the crowd. There was a guy among them. I was pretty sure he was in charge, because he was wearing this big necklace around his neck. I was hoping his name wasn't Jim Jones or anything. Whatever his name was, I wasn't going anywhere near the Kool-Aid. The pair of them embraced and I was sure, if nothing else, that he and my mom had the same Facebook status.

Gross.

A moment later, my body started moving again. I was beginning to hate this. Okay, I'd been hating it for a while now, but I was extra hating it now. I didn't like it when people decided things for me, and I wasn't even getting to choose if I wanted to put up a fight. This sucked.

"He didn't even train her..." my mother was telling the guy. She sounded like she was about to cry. That's okay. I was on my way there, too.

The guy she was clinging to was pretty average looking. He had brown hair, hazel eyes, and a tall and slender build. He wasn't attractive, but then again, after having been around the boys for the past month, who would I consider attractive anymore?

The rest of the group watched me like I was a freak. That was nice of them.

I knew a decent amount about cults. The joys of anthropology was that you learned a heck of a lot about subcultures and fringe groups since they were the really interesting parts of your very own culture. Cults were all about taking away your identity and making you a pawn in some manipulative dude's (and yeah, it was almost always a dude) personal fanatic daydreams.

"Shhh," the man said, wrapping his arms around my mom. He gave me a look, and I felt an immediate need for the world's hottest shower. It was worthy of every creep in every subway that there had ever been. It was as if he looked past my skin to everything that lay beneath. "Welcome to The Homestead, Lorena."

Yup. This was totally a cult. Neat. He said Homestead like it deserved capital letters, like there ought to be rituals held in a creepy basement. I wondered if he had multiple brides, or if he was just waiting for the right group of doe-eyed, not-quite-legals to show up for him to pick from. Well, he could keep his skeevy eyes to himself. I already had enough men in my life.

When I didn't say or do anything, he gave me another look, this one less creepy but no less invasive. "Flower? Is she under your control?"

Flower? Was that my mom's cult name? What were they going to try to name me? Cookie? Honey? Something else sweet and uber-feminine? No, thanks. I'd stick with Lorena.

"She tried to run," my mom said. "She didn't want to come with me."

He gave her a slight tsk and took her face between long fingered hands. "That's not how we do things here, Flower. You know that." He gave her forehead a kiss I might have called tender and then reached a hand out towards me. A moment later, all of my muscles were mine again. He bowed his head. "Forgive your mother, Lorena, she was...overzealous."

"She's a necromancer," my mother whispered, but it was loud enough that I could hear it.

154

Everyone, save for creepy dude, took a step back from me. My mother even shuffled away. Nothing like feeling like the weirdo in a group of cultists.

He eyed me with interest. "Is that so?"

I shrugged. "Maybe? I dunno. I just heard about all of this, you know, right before I was kidnapped against my will."

He waved his hand again. Now that I was all my own self, I could feel the sudden sweep of magic around me. I had begun to notice that everyone's magic felt a little different. Jenny's, who I was most familiar with, had a steady strength to it.

That made sense, because Jenny was pretty much the steadiest person I knew. Connie's magic felt a little...wilder. The guy? His magic felt...old. You know that feeling when you walk into a museum, or a massive forest? It was like that, ethereal and mystic. The car turned back on, the wrought iron fence swung open.

"You are welcome to leave, Lorena. No one will try to stop you. I swear it."

I hesitated for just a second. "What's the catch?"

His chuckle was light and charming. His eyes twinkled. He went from average dude to kinda-cute, and I wondered if that was natural or magical. It didn't really matter; he still skeeved me. "No catch. I would, of course, ask you to hear us out."

"About what?"

"About the prophecy," my mother interrupted. Her eyes were bright with righteous indignation. "You've only heard one side of it! You could-"

The man placed a hand on my mom's shoulder, and she quieted. She turned her head towards him and started to whimper something under very sudden tears. I have to admit, I was a little freaked out. I

155

wasn't one of those chicks who thought that women always had to be strong, that they were never allowed to turn to a friend or loved one and sob out their feelings, but I was always a little leery of the ones who clung to their lovers. A person, dude or chick, ought to be able to stand on their own from time to time. As far as I could tell, the only decision my mom had made so far that day was to kidnap me...and that wasn't really counting in her favor.

Even so, I found myself asking, "What about the prophecy?"

"Why don't we go inside?" he asked, patting my mother's hair as she continued to whimper. "You're mother needs rest."

I frowned. I looked up at the house that looked more like a fortress than anything else. I glanced at the SUV, still humming, and the open gate. I could leave right now; at least, I thought I could. All I had to do was swing myself into the driver's seat and navigate my butt back to familiar territory. Heck, I wanted to do just that. But...but what did he know about the prophecy? What hold did he have on my mother? What was going on?

I had always needed to understand the 'why' of things, even when it got me into trouble.

However, I wasn't completely stupid. I jumped in the SUV and took the keys out of the ignition. My little black dress, cute as it was, did not come with pockets. Curse women's clothing designers. I took off my tassel necklace and added the key to the chain. It ruined the look, but I no longer cared.

"Okay," I said flatly. "Lead the way."

The group, all of us, headed inside the great big scary building. I didn't know a whole lot about architecture, but it looked like a perfect gray box. There were slits of windows, equal in distance from one side of the building to the other. I didn't have a ruler, but I was ninety-five percent positive that the door was in the exact center of the first floor. OCD much?

The inside was just as perfect as the outside. It was nothing like the vampire mansion. Sure, they might have been as equally large, but that was where the similarities ended. The place that I had called home for the past month was all rich wood floors and pretty paintings and warmth. This house was...cold. The walls were stark white. The ground was covered in the same cheap gray carpet you saw in equally cheap apartments. There weren't many pictures on the walls, and what pictures there were would have made M. C. Escher fanboy. I was lead to a room with a big square table that had twenty seats equally distant around the edges.

Yeah, this house was a little...much.

Everyone moved like they were part of some play that I hadn't rehearsed for. They all took seats around the table, and one was left open. Belatedly, I plopped down.

"So..." I said, when the room remained quiet, "nice place you have here. Lots of...squares."

"Magic needs rules, Lorena," my mother said in her best mother-knows-best tone yet. I was impressed, or I would have been if she wasn't still holding on to Creepy Dude's shoulder.

I blinked. I was aware that magic had rules, but I wasn't entirely sure that it needed them. Those felt like two different things. "Oookay," I said, crossing my arms over my chest.

"What your mother means is that there is a Law of Magic, and that you've been...breaking that."

If he was hoping to win me over with this, he had another thing coming. "You wanna...explain that one to me?"

He smiled at me, and I felt an urge to punch him in the face. It wasn't a nice smile or even a welcoming one. It was the kind of smile a person gave a kid when they'd just said something adorably naive.

"You've been learning lesser magic," he said softly. "The magic of mountain witches."

He said 'witches' the way I said 'jerk'. I tried my best to be like Alan, keep my face neutral and politely interested, but I was beginning to feel defensive, maybe even upset. Getting kidnapped could do that to a person.

"Uh-huh," I prompted.

"It is best to picture magic like a great grid work, a perfect pattern of lines equidistant from one another." He placed his hand on the table, and magic swelled around the room. For a second, nothing happened, and then the rest of the group, me excluded, placed one of their hands on the table, palms flat, hands down. A globe blossomed in the middle of the table. It didn't look particularly magical, even though I could feel the magic coming off of it like a breeze. It looked sorta futuristic. "In the best of times, these lines were the same size, shape, and thickness across the world. They cross at exact intervals, and they allow magic to freely flow over the world."

A perfect grid popped up over the globe they had conjured.

I looked around at all the perfectly geometric patterns in the room and was beginning to see a pattern of my own here. "Okay."

It didn't match what I had seen. I had seen a weave of magic, kaleidoscopes of colors that ran through everything, but who was I to say that everyone had to experience the world exactly as I did? That seemed kinda crappy.

"Those who are more...frivolous...in their studies have disrupted that. Their unstable magic has caused the grid to swell in some places, or be completely nonexistent in others. It is what has caused the predicament that we are in."

The lines on the globe moved, sliding from one place to another until the world looked more like a kid trying to draw straight, even lines without a ruler.

For a full twenty seconds, I thought this dude was messing with me. I thought he was going to break out in some big cheesy smile and tell me that he was just joking...but he continued to watch me with a level gaze that made me wish I was wearing the same gray robe to blend in with everyone else.

"The...low magic...predicament?" I said, because I couldn't think of anything else.

"Yes, which brings us to the prophecy." He sighed and stood up. The globe remained in place, slowly revolving. "This idea that you will, by virtue of a child, bring magic back."

"Lemme guess. You don't interpret it that way."

His eyebrow darted up his forehead, his features all shifting to mild confusion.

I held up my hands. I was quickly approaching done. "Dude, let me tell you a thing. I've played this game. I've read this comic. Pretty sure there are like...a thousand movies with this in them. You've got a prophecy, and two or more groups who interpret it differently, and everyone is fighting to see that it turns out in the way that benefits them most, am I right?"

"I-"

I stood up. "Of course, I am. So why don't you tell me what you think I should be doing with myself? Because let me tell you, I looooove being told that. It's my favorite thing."

I sent him a look I hoped was as full of the frustrated disgust I was currently feeling. Tonight was supposed to be fun. It was supposed to be relaxing. Heck, it very nearly was until everyone got involved. Crap like this was why I stayed home on Friday nights.

"Well, that's just it. We don't want you to do anything."

Okay, that one threw me. "What?"

"They want me to."

I don't know what I expected, which had been the theme of my life recently, but it certainly wasn't to turn around and find Connie standing there. She was still wearing her jeans and a tank top. Her riot of hair curling around her freckled face. For a split second, I was absolutely ecstatic to see her. I thought, for some reason, that my buddy was here to rescue me. Then, the full weight of her words hit me like a Mac truck.

"Wait...what?" Then, it hit me. I knew her face had looked familiar. It looked a little like mine. "Holy crap."

"Lorena, this is your sister, Connie. She's your twin," my mother sounded so proud of herself, like she'd just made the perfect soufflé or something. "Well...half-sister."

I blinked in confusion. Wait, was that even possible? Could a woman actually...you know what...why was I questioning that? Like, there was magic in the world; I was sure that there were a billion things that were possible regardless of what science said.

"You?" I asked dumbly.

"What?" she asked. "Did you think you were the only one?"

Well, yes, but I didn't say that out loud. No one had ever told me that I had a sister. No one had ever even insinuated that could have been a thing. I didn't know if I was lied to or if no one knew.

"Okay, back up. What?"

"The prophecy that Loretta gave said that my daughter would give birth to the child of magic. That the child would be born of the blood of a son of Vlad."

I didn't like that phrasing...that sounded bad. "What?"

160

Connie barely even glanced my direction as she walked around the table and stood next to Creepy Dude, who still hadn't bothered to tell me his name. "You said you didn't want to have the child. I do. I know magic better than you. I've been training for this all my life."

Yeah, okay. That might be true. There was even a part of me that was totally down for passing the pressure of having the magic-baby off to someone else, but, to quote the king of all nerd movies, I had a bad feeling about this.

"I really hate to repeat myself, but what's the catch?"

"Don't worry about it," Connie told me.

The very fact that those were the first words out of her mouth had me worrying triple time. But what was I supposed to say – "don't tell me what to do? I'll worry if I want." Somehow, that lacked gumption. "So...you want to have the child?"

She shrugged one freckled shoulder. In her typical non-vocal way, she was answering me.

"What do you want me to do?"

"Go back to your father," my mother said.

Something about this made no sense. My mom had tried really, really hard to get me here. There had been kidnapping involved. Why were they so willing to just let me leave? My spider-sense was totally tingling.

"After Connie gives birth," the Creepy Dude amended.

Ahh, there it was. They weren't willing to leave everything in the hands of fickle fate, were they? Nope. They wanted to lock me up in their citadel of doom for the next nine months. "Is she pregnant?"

"Not yet."

161

Make that a year. I mean, she had to get one of the vampire guys to fall for her. Maybe that wouldn't take too long. I was pretty picky. Then again, maybe she didn't care if they liked her. They wanted magic in the world, too. Right?

"Great," I said. "Imprisoned again. This time without hot dudes."

"Lorena," my mother started. I held up a hand.

"Don't. Like...just don't. It's pretty much bad enough that you weren't in my life, but to find out you've been pretty active in the life of the sister I didn't know I had is enough for a Maury Povich-Dr. Phil crossover show that I really don't need. And you know what? I can't leave if you don't really want me to, even if Creepy Dude over there promises that I can."

"Who? Oh, Markus." My mom offered him a smile.

"Sure, whatever." I shook my head and sighed. "With the ability to take over my body...I know I'm stuck here, so why doesn't one of you gray-clad freaks show me to my room-slash-prison so I can get the hell out of these shoes before this becomes an episode of Jerry Springer?"

My humor, apparently, was lost on them. It was my mother who came over eventually and led me out of the room. I followed her, because I knew that trying to run away was stupid, and it might ruin my plans for later.

Instead, I worked on memorizing the layout as best as I could. It was both easy and difficult. Most houses had different-sized rooms to use up the space in a way that was useful as well as pretty. This one seemed to have a whole other purpose in mind. Every room I saw was pretty much the same size as the room with the table. The bathrooms were more like the showers for gym or something, stalls and such.

"Why is everything so perfect?" I asked.

"Because that is the way of magic," she answered.

"That's not what I've learned."

"You are wrong."

Yeah, I thought, *definitely a mom.* Showed favoritism towards one of her kids and pretended like the other was absolutely screwed.

"So what kind of witch are you?" I asked.

She whirled on me suddenly, her robes becoming a swirl of gray. "I am not a witch. I'm a wizard."

I blinked. Maybe it was the Harry Potter talking, but were witches girls and wizards dudes? Wait...no, that wasn't right. Someone had already told me that witch meant both boy and girl and anything in between. So... what the heck was a wizard?

"I'm sorry," I said, trying to sound a lot more apologetic than I felt. "I don't understand."

She softened instantly. She reached a hand out and touched my cheek. "No, of course you don't. Maybe you can still learn. They haven't ruined you completely. Witches are...wild...chaotic. They just use the magic of the things around them. Their rituals are spontaneous, doing whatever feels right. They have no rules at all."

I didn't think that was completely fair. Witchcraft had plenty of rules, but yeah, a lot of it had to do with intuition. I'd been sort of fumbling with that, but it seemed to be working for others. "But wizardry is different?"

"Oh, yes," her face lit up with the fanaticism that could only be matched by a Cumberbatch fangirl. "Magic ritual, Lorena, is rules and meaning."

I nodded. I mean, I wasn't completely disinterested. I hadn't actually been doing all that great with the intuitive magic...at least, until tonight I hadn't. "Will you show me?"

She gave me a funny look, like she didn't quite believe me. I wasn't lying, not totally. "Why?"

I shrugged. "I mean, I want to know about magic. I want to learn, to understand."

She put a hand on my cheek. "Of course, you do. But not tonight, it's late."

Well, that much was true. I was tired, my feet hurt, and if everything went the way I wanted it to, it was going to be a very long night. I nodded. "Alright."

She turned around and continued to lead me. At the end of the hall was a room. I could tell that ten people could have lived in there, it had enough bunk beds for it, but there were no robes or anything personal hung about. The shelves between the beds were empty. I was guessing there weren't many little wizards to join up.

I plopped down on a bed.

"I know it doesn't seem like it right now, Lorena, but this is for the best."

I wondered if my mom knew how much she sounded like every villain ever drawn. Probably not. "Yeah."

"Rest, we will talk more tomorrow."

I tugged off my heels and flopped over, and proceeded to count to one hundred. The moment I did, I jumped up and went right to the door. I was going to do the simplest escape ever. Just walk right out the front door and drive the SUV through that wrought iron fence.

I put my hand on the doorknob and tugged. Nothing happened. I tugged again...and again...and again. All of the time had about the same effect. This wasn't the normal tugging on a locked door. This was more like pulling on a brick wall. Nothing moved. Great.

It didn't take a genius to realize that I had been magically imprisoned. Frick. Double frick. What was I supposed to do now? My super simple escape plan had been thwarted by a door. I began to look around the room, trying to find all the normal escapes. A vent big enough for a chubby girl to squirm through. A ceiling tile that would let me up. Nothing. I was beginning to touch every available surface, looking for the secret door switch, when I heard a whisper of movement in the hallway. A moment later, the door opened and a girl peeked her head in.

I didn't recognize her from the group that met me at the front door. I had assumed that they had been the entire cult. Apparently, I was wrong. She was a pretty girl. She had deep olive skin and eyes the color of honey. Her black hair was pulled into a long braid. She wore the same gray robe as everyone else, but it didn't seem to fit her right. The size was okay, but it didn't suit her.

"Are you the girl from the prophecy?"

Well, that wasn't as easy to answer as it had been half an hour ago. But I said yes anyway.

"Follow me."

It was tempting to just shut up and do what she said...but I had never been one for just doing what I was told. "Who are you?"

"My name is Reika. I'm here to rescue you."

"My very own Stormtrooper."

She gave me a funny look. "What?"

"Never mind...why?"

She sighed. "Do you really want to know that right now?"

"Well...yes. Sorry, but it's been a weird night."

"Because I want to get out of this place, and you are how I can do it."

Ah, see, that I understood. She wasn't in this just to be nice and rescue the girl she didn't know; she wanted to get away from the creepy gray robed cult, too. That I believed. "Alright, let's go."

She handed me a gray robe, and I tugged it on. I didn't like it. It was itchy. We pulled up the hoods, and she tugged me until I was standing right next to her. I followed in her footsteps, trying to be as quiet as possible. She was looking down at the floor, so I did, too.

"Keep your eyes on your feet; try to look normal," Reika told me.

I had not, in my entire life, looked normal. Typical or able-bodied, sure, but not normal. "Okay."

I was trying really, really hard to be absolutely normal when I felt something. It was hard to describe. It was like something was tugging at my mind or my spirit, or maybe a little of both. I turned my head and looked down the hallway that I was almost sure the sensation was coming from. I wanted to ignore it. I knew that it would be smarter to, but the moment that I felt it, I knew that I had to go find out what was happening.

I was walking down the hallway before I even realized I had fully made the decision. Reika grabbed my arm and tried to tug me back. "Where are you going?"

"This way...I have to."

I swear it made perfect sense to me at the time. When Reika started to hiss that I was being an idiot, I knew she was right, but I knew that I couldn't ignore it either.

"Seriously, I have to," I said.

She frowned at me. "You are going to ruin my chance for escape."

"Go on, then. I'll meet you at the door."

She didn't believe me. To be fair, I didn't believe me either. I was pretty sure that I was about to walk into the trappiest trap that ever trapped, but what was I supposed to do? Ignoring it just didn't seem to be an option. I walked, and Reika followed.

"We aren't supposed to be down here," she whispered at me. I was getting the feeling that my rescuer was also a bit of a worrywart.

"We aren't supposed to be breaking out of here either, but that doesn't seem to be bothering you."

She smiled. See, at least someone in this complex thought I was funny.

I ignored all the doors along the hall until we got to the very last one. Of course, it was. It couldn't be something normal like the first door on the right. It had to be all the way at the end of this place that was so boringly white and geometric that it was almost impossible to navigate.

"What's in there?" she asked.

"I don't know...but I need to find it."

I tugged on the door. It didn't open. She pushed me aside. I let her. Hey, she knew more about this place than I did. She tugged out a container made of dark wood. She unscrewed it, and the scent of chalk filled the air. It was blue and stood out on her fingers as she began to draw a perfect circle on the door. She bisected it with lines so perfect I'd have needed a ruler and a prayer to accomplish them. Then, she added symbols that I didn't understand. The next thing I knew, magic surged out and the door opened.

167

"What the heck was that?" I wanted to know.

She shot me a look. "Wizardry."

Right. Of course. What had I been thinking?

The room was as boringly decorated as the rest of the place, but that wasn't what caught my attention. In the very middle of the room was a bed, and in that bed was a man. He was tall and brown-skinned. His head was perfectly shaved, and a series of tattoos were imprinted on the flesh. There was an attractiveness to his features, high strong cheekbones and good form, but it was all muted by the fact that he looked like he had been bled dry...which wasn't too far from the truth.

A strange apparatus was hooked up to him. It had needles sticking into his skin and there were like...six jars sitting at six equal points inside of a circle that was made of what I could only assume was blood.

"Holy crap," I said.

Reika tugged on my arm. "We need to go."

"I'm not leaving someone like that!" I said, all full of righteous indignation.

"He's already dead."

I blinked. How could she say that? I could feel that he was alive I could... "He's a vampire...oh my god...that's Zane."

"Who?"

I knew it had to be. It had to be the last of the four sons of Vlad. He was a vampire. That's why I knew he was alive. Check one in the pro column for necromancy. "We have to get him out of here."

"Why?"

"Because if we don't, then Connie gets to have the prophecy baby."

She gave me another funny look. "You don't want her to? I heard-"

"Listen, I've got a lot of mixed feelings. Sue me. But one thing I am not cool with is tying up a person in your bedroom and sucking them dry. Like...I don't know a lot about magic...but killing something to make yours happen doesn't seem like a great idea."

"You don't know they are killing him. It's a vampire."

"Yeah, I do."

I knew. I did. I knew it in a way I couldn't entirely explain. Call it witchcraft, call it intuition. But I was absolutely one hundred percent sure that this was hurting him. I was sure what I felt was his undead soul calling out for me. I surged forward just as Reika said "Wait!"

The magic surged towards me and then through me, tossing me back against the far wall with so much force I was left breathless. It did not feel good. Not even a little bit.

The vampire turned his head in my direction. "Help."

"Working on it," I gasped out. I charged forward, my ribs aching. "I need to get into this circle thing."

"We should go. Someone will have heard that." She was looking down the hall, as if waiting for people to suddenly appear. I hadn't heard anything, but the pulse of magic was strong enough that other people might have felt something. Was that the same thing? Maybe Reika actually heard magic when I just felt it. I didn't know. Magic was weird.

I took a deep breath, deep enough that it hurt my already tender body. I looked at the guy laid out and half dead...re-dead...more dead? I didn't know. I just knew that I absolutely could not leave him like that. "Please?"

She frowned, but she began drawing symbols in the bloody circle, her lips twisted in dislike.

The magic shuddered as she added her own to it, and I waited. I let my eyes gloss over until I could see the lines of the Weave as they worked in this room. The lines were...well, they were certainly more orderly here. They followed perfect paths regardless of what they were moving through. When I had seen them before, they seemed to follow the lines of nature and carpentry. Here, it was like everything had been built around them. It made me vaguely uncomfortable.

Several of the lines were focused into the circle, pushing into the vampire that I was assuming was Zane. They didn't look like normal magic lines...they looked spiky, like they were supposed to hurt. Lines were pouring out of him too, filling up the six jars. This all felt strange and wrong and I didn't like it at all.

"They are coming!" Reika hissed.

I didn't ask who. I could guess.

"Hurry!" I told her.

The magic broke, and I surged forward, plucking out the tubes from his body. He gasped, but not because he needed to breathe. It just hurt. A moment later, my mother and Connie and several of the gray-robed wizards were all pouring into the room. Oh, this wasn't good. They radiated magic. Their hands linked, and that power built and focused around me. I could tell they were trying to hold me still. It wasn't working as well as it had before, and I wasn't sure why.

"What's going on here?" my mother wanted to know.

"Gee," I snapped out. "I was pretty sure that was my question. What are you doing to him?"

170

Connie gave me the biggest sneer that I had ever seen. "How else do you make a baby with blood?"

Okay. Ew. Not cool. I didn't want to know any more. "We are leaving."

My mother shook her head. "No, you aren't."

I wanted to say something cool, like "try and stop me," but that was when I heard a great big commotion going on downstairs. Their heads turned, and I shouted, "Run!"

Zane couldn't run, not on his own. He was too weak and drained. He tried though, bless him. His long legs struggled to try to get under him. I put one arm around him, but I wasn't tall enough or strong enough to be of much help.

"Help him!" Reika shouted over her shoulder, trying to dart through the doorway.

"Trying!"

"Some necromancer you are," Connie sneered.

That, quite possibly, was the most helpful thing that anyone had ever said to me. I'd played enough video games to know that necromancers were all about the undead. Sure, the flavor of that connection differed from one thing to the next, but undead were totally their jam. I remembered the power pouring into the jars, and I focused on it.

The power jumped to me, rushed into me. I felt like I'd exercised every day of my life and had just gotten done with my most recent world tour of martial arts. I was strong, fast, powerful...but I knew the power wasn't mine. With nothing but my force of will, I shoved all that power into Zane, and he damn near jumped.

This was why their magic wasn't working as well, I realized. It didn't matter that their lines of magic were all perfectly laid out. Blood was on the ground, and that was the essence of life energy. That was necromancy, and it was all mine. Well, okay, it was Zane's...but still.

One moment he was leaning on me, the next he was moving. I had Wei to compare him to, and Dmitri for that matter. I knew that vampires could be fast. I just didn't expect the blur of motion that left three wizards on the ground and me scooped up in a pair of slender arms. The next thing I knew, we were downstairs, and Reika was on our tail. The front door was open.

"Wow," she whispered to herself. I was feeling pretty much the same. I had expected an epic boss battle, lots of magic being flung this way and that. Instead, all I had gotten was a blur of commotion. I'd complain about it later.

I was just about to walk out the front door when I heard the last thing that I expected.

"Lorena!"

"Wei!" I cried out, completely shocked.

The room where the cult and I had gone about our little conversation was a wreck. Markus stood in the center of it. His entire body glowed with circles of magic, tattooed into the skin, which had been covered by his gray robe earlier. Circles upon circles of interconnected glyphs glimmered against his skin. The power that rolled off of him was so much that my ribs, already tender, screamed with painful indignation.

Wei had his sword in hand, still wearing the jeans and the t-shirt that he had been wearing at the club, but both were soaked with blood. I hadn't even known that vampires could bleed. Wounds were visible on his flesh, but I didn't know what had made them. To one side was Alan, gripping his stomach, leaning heavily against the wall, and to the other was Dmitri...or at least, I thought it was Dmitri. He looked...well, he looked more like a massive man-bear than the boy I had grown to care about. Wei was bloodied, and his eyes were a shock of red.

"What are you doing here?" I demanded.

"Rescuing you."

"No!" Markus shouted, and the word was filled with arcane power. The room seemed to shake with it. I had never felt anything like it, even from Marquesa. "You will go nowhere. I will not have magic running rampant through the world. I will not have it!"

That sounded...weird. What else was magic supposed to do?

"Let us go!"

He shook his head and raised his hands in the air. I knew that he was going to do something terrible, so I did the only thing I could do. I stole magic. I stole it from Alan, from Dmitri, from Zane. I stole parts of that essence that made them what they were, and I shoved it into Wei. Wei, who I knew could be so strong. Wei, who I knew to be the most powerful of the sons of Vlad. I poured it into him like water into a cup. I filled him with everything that I could, and when he couldn't take any more, the magic flashed back into me. Oops.

For a moment, I couldn't see what happened; instead, all I could see was my face. It wasn't like looking in the mirror; it was softer than what I saw. It was my smile, my rolling eyes, the way my jeans hugged my legs. It was me trying my best at martial arts and me practicing magic. Visions of me reading quietly in the library, or me chatting amiably with Peter.

An image of me, lounging at the club, with my black dress stretched across the thickness of my thighs. My lips, smothered in red. There were a lot of other images of me, too, things I knew that Wei had never seen, lusty things...hungry ones. It was me the way Wei saw me, and it was so full of love and lust that I was struck breathless by it.

Then again, maybe that was the cracked ribs.

When my vision finally cleared, I was struck dumb again, but for a completely other reason. The room, which had already been a mess, was a complete wreck. The table was in pieces, shattered as if it had exploded from the inside out. Alan had Dmitri's head in his lap, whispering something soothing in French. A large piece of wood was sticking out of Dmitri's shoulder. Alan jerked as a piece of wood as long as my arm struck him in the back.

It was then that I realized Markus was trying to stake my vampires. Hey. Not cool. Not cool at all. I glanced around and saw Zane, still exhausted and gray around the eyes, leaning heavily against the door frame, doing his best not to be a target.

My eyes landed on Wei. He was bloody again, but his body was moving so fast I could barely see it. His blade was a glimmer of silver as it lashed and struck. Markus, somehow, was keeping up. The blade in his hands was made of magic, invisible until Wei's blade made contact with it, then it would shine.

Markus slammed his hand outward, and Wei went flying across the room. I really hated that trick; it had happened to me too often tonight.

"Hey!" I shouted. Markus' head jerked in my direction. "What the hell is wrong with you?"

"You are!" he shouted. I don't think I'd ever heard anything so bitter.

"What the heck did I ever do to you?"

His eyes lit up with long swallowed anger. "You were born." He came after me then. He moved fast, almost vampire fast, which was a lot quicker than I was able to. I stumbled back, and his magic blade cut into the wall to my left. "Everything would have been fine. Connie would have already birthed the child were it not for you."

I had no idea what he meant by that. As far as I knew, I had done absolutely nothing to disrupt any of that. I hadn't even known it was going on. That was fine though. He could think that. If he kept his

174

attention on me, Wei could make the final strike. I didn't dare look, but I knew it was coming. Wei loved me...he would keep me safe.

"You're nuts."

"You're worthless!" he spat back.

As far as comebacks go, that one lacked oomph. "Try again."

"The ritual was almost ready," he snarled, swinging the blade again. It was a wild swing, and I jumped back, but I wasn't quite fast enough. The invisible blade caught me across the chest, cutting from my hip to my belly button. It did not feel good. It was like the world's worst razor slicing through my skin. Fire-hot pain ripped through me.

"Hey!" I shouted out. "That's my dress!"

Yeah, that was my biggest thought right then. My priorities are not perfect. He was a little shocked, too. He went totally still with confusion, and that moment was all Wei needed. His blade struck out like a blur of silver and buried itself in Markus' side. He jerked the blade out and slammed it in again. Wei's face was contorted with anger.

"No!" My mother's scream was shrill and unexpected, but not as unexpected as the wave of energy that rolled off of Markus.

"Wei, get Alan!" I yelled. I turned my attention to Dmitri. I did something I hated. I manipulated his body the same way my mom had manipulated mine. If Dmitri hadn't been a vampire, it wouldn't have worked...but I managed to get all of us out of there and into the SUV. I didn't even feel my cut.

I didn't think about anything else, not what the power spilling behind me like a typhoon meant, or where Jenny was, or anything. I just shoved the key still dangling around my neck into the ignition. My necklace broke, and I didn't care. The engine roared to life, and I slammed my bare foot to the gas and shot us out of there.

When I looked into the mirror, my mother was standing on the porch, Markus sagging against her left, Connie, the sister I never knew I had, on her right. I knew this wasn't over. Not by a long shot.

THE FINAL CHAPTER

On the way home, I told them everything that I had found out, and they told me what they knew. Yes, the man I had rescued was Zane. Yes, they knew wizards existed, but they hadn't known that any were here. I heard most of it, but I was tired and worried and I think a little drunk on magic.

"We are The Ordo Hermeticus Fidelis," Reika explained. "The Order of the Loyal Hermit. An ancient order of magic that has been around for many centuries."

She said it with real pride, which I thought was kind of strange since she had been so intent on getting the heck out of there. So far as I could tell, the order wasn't very nice. "Didn't seem very hermit-y to me," I said, remembering the slew of people there.

"We study individually, but practice as a whole. Or at least, we used to before Markus took over as the order's leader. He...he wants to be worshiped. He ruins what the order ought to be."

That I could believe. I hadn't known him for very long, fifteen minutes, max, but I got the feeling that Reika was absolutely right. He had the perfect woman on one side and Connie on the other. She was his daughter, Reika told me. I wasn't surprised by that, I had already expected it.

"We aren't bad," she promised, "We simply believe in the order of magic. That it shouldn't be practiced by just anyone, that you need to earn the right to its power."

I frowned. "Sounds kinda high-minded to me. Like...classist magic."

She gave me a look that said I was being stupid. "You can do more with magic than you can with a gun. Do you want everyone in the world to have a gun?"

I didn't have a lot of hard fast rules on the subject of gun control other than 'I don't think bad people should have them.' "That doesn't feel fair," I finally said. "A gun is just a weapon; its only use is to hurt something. Magic can heal and stuff, too."

She sighed and rolled her eyes. I could see that this was a conversation she'd had before and didn't want to have again. That was fine. I didn't want to have it either. I had a lot to think about. "The Order is afraid that if you, a practitioner of witchcraft, has the child, then that will flavor the magic that the world receives."

I sighed. "Ah, this isn't the good vs. evil prophecy; this is the law vs. chaos one. Got it."

"You are strange."

There was a chorus of laughter from the men. Even Wei. No, I realized, especially Wei. He loved me. I was absolutely sure of that. His slight chuckle was another man's belly laugh. His small flick of interest was equal to my squeal of fangirl delight. He loved me, and I think he had from the beginning.

"You're also bleeding," Reika said, pointing to my side.

"Shoot," I said, remembering the cut I had received. That last gush of adrenaline was fading, and with Reika's words, it was disappearing entirely. "Yeah...I am."

"Pull over," Wei said. "I will drive."

I glanced over my shoulder and then pulled off so that we could switch places. He paused long enough to touch my shoulder. His eyes were like black fire inside his handsome face. His hair was a mess. "You did well."

I felt a strange flutter in my stomach. Maybe it was adrenaline. Yeah, I was going to blame that. I cleared my throat and nodded before taking a spot next to Alan. His arm went around my shoulders and I took it for the comfort that he intended it to be. Dmitri, who I knew he cared about, was laying across the seat with his head in Alan's lap.

"So," Alan said, "this changes things."

"Changes what?" I asked.

"You need to choose your partner," Wei said from the front seat. "And you need to choose now."

Oh, right. That....

To Be Continued.....

* * *

Ready for the next part of the story?

Dear Reader,

I want to personally thank you for taking your time to read "***House Of Vampires***" I really hope you enjoyed it and you are hungry for the next part in the story.

"House Of Vampires 2" is available to pre-order now and if you do so you get it for 99c instead of $2.99 so if you want to it delivered to your device on release date then follow the link below and pre-order right away!

PRE-ORDER HOUSE OF VAMPIRES 2

See you in the next book :)

Samantha x x

Get Yourself a FREE Bestselling Paranormal Romance Book!

Join the "**Simply Shifters**" Mailing list today and gain access to an exclusive **FREE** classic Paranormal Shifter Romance book by one of our bestselling authors along with many others more to come. You will also be kept up to date on the best book deals in the future on the hottest new Paranormal Romances. We are the HOME of Paranormal Romance after all!

* Get FREE Shifter Romance Books For Your Kindle & Other Cool giveaways

* Discover Exclusive Deals & Discounts Before Anyone Else!

* Be The FIRST To Know about Hot New Releases From Your Favorite Authors

Click The Link Below To Access Get All This Now!

SimplyShifters.com

Already subscribed?
OK, *Turn The Page!*

ALSO BY SIMPLY SHIFTERS....

SIMPLY VAMPIRES
A TEN BOOK VAMPIRE ROMANCE COLLECTION

99c or FREE to read with Kindle Unlimited

This unique 10 book package features some of the best selling authors from the world of Paranormal Romance. The perfect blend of love, sex and adventure involving curvy, cute heroines and their handsome vampire lovers.

Book 1 - JJ Jones – The White Vampire
Book 2 – Samantha Snow – A Lighter Shade Of Pale
Book 3 - Amira Rain – Melted By The Vampire
Book 4 - Serena Rose – Prince Lucien
Book 5 – Ellie Valentina – Red Solstice
Book 6 - Bonnie Burrows – The Vampire's Shared Bride
Book 7 - Jade White – Never Have A Vampires Baby
Book 8 - Angela Foxxe – A Billion Secrets
Book 9 - Samantha Snow - Spawn Of The Vampire
Book 10 - Jasmine White – Bitten By The Bad Boy

TAP HERE TO DOWNLOAD THIS NOW!

Made in the USA
Coppell, TX
09 November 2022